D1542246

THE IMAGINARY LIVES OF MECHANICAL MEN

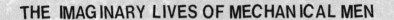

THE IMAGINARY LIVES
OF MECHANICAL MEN
STORIES BY RANDY F. NELSON

The University of Georgia Press   *Athens & London*

Published by the University of Georgia Press
Athens, Georgia 30602
© 2006 by Randy F. Nelson

Designed by Erin Kirk New
Set in 9.8 on 14 Electra
Printed and bound by Thomson-Shore

The paper in this book meets the guidelines for
permanence and durability of the Committee on
Production Guidelines for Book Longevity of the
Council on Library Resources.

Printed in the United States of America
06 07 08 09 10 C 5 4 3 2 1

Library of Congress Cataloging-in-Publication Data
Nelson, Randy F., 1948–
    The imaginary lives of mechanical men : stories by / Randy F. Nelson.
        p. cm. — (Winner of the Flannery O'Connor Award for Short Fiction)
    ISBN-13: 978-0-8203-2845-4 (hardcover : alk. paper)
    ISBN-10: 0-8203-2845-6 (hardcover : alk. paper)
    I. Title. II. Flannery O'Connor Award for Short Fiction.
    PS3614.E4493I43   2006
    813'.6—dc22   2005037661

British Library Cataloging-in-Publication Data available

for my family

Contents

Acknowledgments

The author and the publisher gratefully acknowledge the journals in which many of the stories in this collection first appeared: "Abduction" in *North American Review*; "Breaker" in *Glimmer Train*; "The Cave" in *Crazyhorse*; "Cutters" in *Story*; "Escape" in *Georgia Review*; "Food Is Fuel" in *Seattle Review*; "The Guardian" in *Gettysburg Review*; "Here's a Shot of Us at the Grand Canyon" in *Kenyon Review*; "In the Picking Room" in *Portland Review*; "Pulp Life" in *Northwest Review*; "Refiner's Fire" in *Southern Review*; "River Story" in *Descant*. The quotation from *The Iliad* in "Refiner's Fire" is from Robert Fagles's translation published by Penguin Classics in 1991.

For the language, lore, history, and procedures of shipbreaking, I am indebted to articles and images by William Langewiesche ("The Shipbreakers," *Atlantic*, August 2000) and Edward Burtynsky (www .cowlesgallery.com). For help at all stages of research, I am grateful to the librarians of E. H. Little Library. Thanks also to Alice Tasman of the Jean V. Naggar Literary Agency and especially to Susan Nelson for her continuing assurance and inspiration.

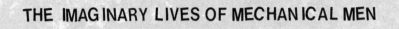

THE IMAGINARY LIVES OF MECHANICAL MEN

Mechanical Men

For every death or serious injury within the compound itself, I write an incident report. This is partly for insurance purposes, partly to establish a database, but mostly to keep outside funds flowing into the Center. After I've written the report, I have it certified by a private investigator then notarized over my signature, with copies getting sent to the funding agencies, individual project directors, and on down through the bureaucracy. It's the way science is done now. Of course if there were more than one death in a relatively short time, then I wouldn't want to use the same investigator twice, would I? It might look like a pattern.

Which is why I called Peggy over at Harris, Helms, and Stillman. She made it sound like she was fronting for a law firm. So it took a while to establish that Stillman wasn't in the office.

"Thank you," I said. "Please just tell him I'll pick him up tomorrow morning at 8:30. I'll be out front. Tan Lexus, four door."

"Are you a client of ours, Mr. Levin?"

"A friend. Just mention my name."

"And what should I tell him it's about?"

"Say it's about the death of a very important chimpanzee."

"Sir?"

"What else can I tell you? I lie for a living."

So the next morning I laid out Janie's meds, helped the home nurse move her up in the bed, and kissed her good-bye as though it were the last time. Just like every morning. Then drove through one of those winter rains that can't seem to rinse the grime off our streets. Potholes overflowing like toilets, and trucks slinging muck over your windshield. Every few blocks I seemed to pass some homeless guy throwing off steam like he'd been boiled for three days. Then a strip mall closed up like an armadillo. Even Stillman's office looked like a burger joint that had failed in the eighties. He was standing out front watching a woman yank her kid toward the bus stop. And I blew the horn just to see if he'd flinch.

He'd always been precise in his movements, like one of those mechanical toys in *Blade Runner*, so I'm not sure what I expected. Maybe for him to rotate his head and look down like I was vermin. Anyhow, he was uncanny enough. There was the scar that you wouldn't notice unless you looked, running from hairline to neck, and the animatronic eyes that you see in deaf people. I wondered if he still had hearing in one ear. He gave the black overcoat a shake and slipped into the front seat beside me. Then I swung a left and headed back into the traffic. It was a minute or two before he spoke. I guess he needed to warm up.

Finally he brought me up to date by saying "Nice weather," dropping the *r* and losing the sibilance altogether. It sounded like *nigh weatha*. So, yeah, I felt great about the horn thing.

"How ya doing?" I said.

"Doing okay. How about you?"

"I'm getting there."

And that's the way we handled it until the years melted away. It took a while. Stillman barely moved his lips, like he was afraid of making a mistake, and maybe I overarticulated a little. But by the time we'd got to the city limits, he felt comfortable enough to say, "How come you talk like a fruit?"

"I enunciate. I'm on TV a lot. How come you're wearing the same coat?"

"Because the disability check sucks."

"You sound good."

"So you do lie. Look, I can still hear if that's what you want to know, 70 percent out of the right ear. I don't use a hearing aid. And I can read your damn mind if I watch your face while you're talking. So I thought we ought to get that part out of the way. In case you were wondering."

"Glad you haven't changed."

"So, anyhow. Where we going?"

"To the Land of Oz."

"*Odz*? Like the movie?"

"Yeah, like someplace you're not going to believe."

"This place got a real name?"

"The Jervis Center. We're about twenty minutes out."

"The monkey place?"

"The Jervis Center for Primate Research. Except the subject of your report is a chimpanzee, named Greta, who was maybe thirty times smarter than any human you know."

"Was?"

"She's dead. And therefore holding up some very expensive research. And idling some very expensive equipment. And inconveniencing some very expensive people. So here's the deal. You get $2,500 to ride out, look around, and sign a report saying how she got dead—submitted on your letterhead. I write the report; you sign it. You got twenty-four hours starting five minutes ago."

"Yeah, well, maybe I ought to get this out of the way too. I don't do insurance fraud."

"It's more complicated than that."

"I get to ask any questions?"

"After we get there and I introduce you around, you can go anywhere you want, ask anything you want. As long as you finish in twenty-three hours and fifty-five minutes."

"Somebody in a hurry?"

"Everybody I know's in a hurry."

He didn't have a comeback for that because he'd been a cop for eighteen years. He already knew. For a few minutes he watched the windshield wipers and the rain snakes crawling on the side window. Then he finally got around to it. "Look. I heard about Janie a few months ago. Sorry."

It sounded like he'd said *Danie*. Like he was trying to be cute.

"I guess it's rough," he said.

"We're getting by."

"She's in one of those, you know, hospital places?"

"Hospice?"

"Yeah."

"Is that your first question? Or are we just killing time?"

I drove us past the protesters in the parking lot and over to the medical wing, where I introduced Stillman to Katharine Woodruff, head of neurology. She was one of the brain busters who made the chimps do arithmetic so they'd develop ulcers and we could thus better understand humanity. Or something like that. Like every vice president I've ever met, she had Stillman's hand before I'd even mentioned his name. He passed her one of his business cards. She slipped it into a folder. He took in the windows, the vaulted ceiling, and the vast, empty spaces of her office like it was his first visit to the cathedral. Which it probably was. And she gave him a moment to look around. It was touching. I could see Stillman trying not to be impressed, trying to be the cop he used to be. Running his knuckles over the top of her desk, like he might be planning to land a helicopter on it. So she gave him a second or two and then said, "Mr. Levin here has explained the protocol?"

"Yeah, I guess. I'm just a little unclear why you need somebody like me."

As he spoke, Katharine focused on his face, attempting to read beneath Stillman's surface. She found the scar and had to prevent herself from touching it.

"Mr. Stillman is slightly hearing impaired," I said. "As the result of an explosion. He was a decorated detective with the NYPD until he had to retire on partial disability, after a bad morning with a suspicious package."

"I'm sorry," she said.

"We knew each other," I went on, "back when I was a reporter. I covered a few of his cases. He's good."

"I see. Well, Mr. Stillman, to answer your question—the local police are out of the picture. This is a private property issue as far as they're concerned. Second, your time, to be honest, is less costly than that of research staff. And, third, our insurers require an outside vetting. Greta was the subject of neuro-cognitive experiments which are vital to a new medical procedure we're hoping to market in a very short . . ."

"You got a monkey who was murdered?"

"Greta was not a monkey, Mr. Stillman. In fact, that's one reason Mr. Levin here will be helping with your report. As assistant director of public relations, he frequently has to translate our language into . . . more public language. Greta, to be precise, was *Pan troglodytes*, an east African chimpanzee and the closest relative to humans in the animal kingdom. Her DNA was 98.4 percent identical to yours."

"But this Greta. She's like 98.4 percent dead now, am I right?"

"Yes."

"You have your own security people?"

"Yes. In the past week they've reported nothing more than a minor break-in and the usual protesters."

"Break-in where?"

"A photography lab. Some lighting equipment and battery packs went missing."

"Protesters?"

"I'm sure you saw them when you came in. Animal rights groups, most of them—PETA, that sort of thing—people who think the animals are being abused. The world is full of romanticists, Mr. Stillman, who believe that science advances by magic or by computer modeling or some such nonsense."

"So are they? Being abused that is?"

Katharine looked at me and then toward the dark mahogany of her twin office doors. "Greta fell, Mr. Stillman. From a high place. Which I'm sure you'd like to examine for yourself. Laurence, if you would perhaps show our guest to the compound itself, you could introduce him to Dr. Deckard on your way."

"Yeah," I said, "that would probably be the best thing."

So we ran the maze.

I took him back to the atrium, across the polished marble, clep-clepping like horses at the bottom of the Grand Canyon. Then into the chrome elevator that they probably don't have in the Grand Canyon, where we watched the numbers flicker and listened to the soft ping of passing floors, all the way up to INFECTIOUS DISEASES. And then down the syringe. That's what they call it on the public tours. A glassed-in hallway—almost a tube—connecting two of the buildings. It gives a spectacular view of the entire campus. Though at night it's a little different. Twelve stories up, you think twice about stepping out into nothing. And even in the daytime it's intimidating.

So halfway across, I stopped him, just to make my point. "In case you're wondering, this isn't a joke. There's a hell of a lot at stake here. So don't get cute with these people."

"Or what? They'll make me stay after school?"

"Just stick with the program, okay?"

"Sure. I figure you're paying better than the government."

In a small anteroom outside a door marked DISSECTION, we put on cleansuits, booties, and masks. Then I keyed the numbers into the security pad. On the other side of the door, a lab assistant checked us out and pointed toward a white-gowned figure manipulating a robotic arm that descended from the ceiling. He looked like a dentist. Other white figures clustered around a stainless steel table in the center of the room. The subject of their attention was not moving.

"Dr. Deckard?" The assistant halted us outside the circle of bowed heads.

"Yes?"

"It's Mr. Levin," the assistant said. "He's here with the vetting officer."

"Laurence. Of course." The dentist-figure glanced at us without standing upright. "Come over and have a look if you want, although I'm afraid you'll be disappointed. This isn't an autopsy. Our only real concern is with the neural pathways and"—he sawed through a bit of skull with a far too familiar sound—"how the connectors performed. But you're welcome to observe. Give us a little more water flow here."

"This is Augustus Stillman," I said. "Dr. Deckard is the lead investigator for the neuro-cognitive section."

"Augustus. An emperor we don't hear from every day." Deckard lifted away a portion of the cranium and laid it in an aluminum pan. "I always thought you got a bum rap in Shakespeare. Caught you at a bad time."

Stillman looked at me.

"He says you got a bum rap. Shakespeare and all that."

"So what kind of experiment was it?"

Something in Stillman's tone caused Deckard to rise up and study us for the first time. He was wearing a plasticine face shield that exaggerated the mantislike features of his face. "Fascinating stuff really. Can you see that? Right down there? The visual cortex. It's where neurons first register motion in the brain. But here's the really interesting thing. You can have tons of visual input and no consciousness at all of motion or form or color or depth or velocity unless everything's connected to the frontal lobes, up here. What that means is that if the wiring's no good, then we don't actually see anything. Makes you wonder what we miss every day, doesn't it?"

"You did something to the wiring in her brain?"

"In a sense. We wanted to know what would happen if we could increase the intensity and speed of her connections, so to speak. Could we create a kind of superconsciousness, at least visually?"

"You were making a genius chimp."

"In a very limited sense. Think of it this way. You, and most humans, can look at a ceiling fan, for example, and after a few minutes it looks as if the blades are rotating backward. Now in reality we know that the blades aren't going backward at all, but it seems that way because our perception is out of sync with what's really happening. So—what would reality look like if we could triple or maybe quadruple the amount of information flowing from cortex to lobes? Human beings just assume that reality is something that *flows* all around them. But what would reality look like to a much faster processor?"

"You sped up Greta's brain."

"We inserted microscopic implants, rerouting a number of neural pathways. Roughly four times the amount of information moving from the visual cortex to the frontal lobes. In some ways, a very simple and elegant procedure."

"So what went wrong?"

"Nothing. At least not procedurally. She had recovered nicely from the operation, and we had just released her back into the compound."

Stillman edged closer to the table and looked at the peaceful figure. It was hard to tell what he was thinking. "She looks like a muppet," he said.

"I never thought of it like that."

"So how did she actually die?"

The question seemed to catch Deckard off guard. He thought a moment and reached behind the cranium so he could move the head in several directions. "Broken neck, I'm afraid."

"That's too bad."

"It's too bad for a lot of people. The same procedure we used on Greta will be used on humans in the very near future. Stroke victims,

Alzheimer's, epilepsy, ALS, cerebral palsy, brain cancer. We already know it will work. What we have to do now is demonstrate that it will work, which is the part of my job that I detest, putting on puppet shows for government review boards. People will die, Mr. Stillman. Real live people will die for every delay we face in this program. Our procedure is that revolutionary. And the animals here at the Jervis Center get the most humane possible treatment. They are very lucky."

"Lucky?"

"Yes, very. If you haven't seen the compound yet, get ready to be amazed."

"I'm already pretty amazed, doctor. So this broken neck. How would you say it came about?"

"She fell. From the top of the escarpment. The tape caught most of it."

"The tape?"

"I should have told you," I said. "We have most of it on camera. Digital, not actual tape. I just thought you'd want to see the compound first, where it actually happened."

"Whatever you say."

On the way out, Deckard asked me how Janie was doing, as if he'd just happened to think of it on the spur of the moment.

I gave him a look. "We're doing okay," I said. "We have a woman who stays during the day. Nurse drops by a few times a week."

"Good. That's good," he said.

I let Stillman go on out into the hall and turned so that I fully faced the bastard. "You don't have to remind me of anything," I said. "I'm handling it."

"I was just concerned. Tell her I was thinking about her."

In the observation room Stillman seemed hypnotized by the birds. On the other side of the glass they were soaring, not flitting or hopping or pacing along branches like pet shop parakeets, but rather soaring inside a biosphere that itself soared higher than an aircraft hangar.

He focused on a flock of yellow bee-eaters, swarming like mosquitoes and then diving into the greenery below us. After a while he said, "I thought this place was for monkeys."

"It's a complete ecosystem. What you can see from here is the south-east quadrant. Three streams, two waterfalls. A lake. Fish, birds, anthills. Orchids. Strangler vines. Everything that's endemic to the animals' environment. Four point two acres of habitat completely enclosed and rigorously managed. Twice as large as the original Biosphere project in Arizona, except that this one works. Outside the compound itself there's another 317 acres accommodating 18 different primate species within 31 large social enclosures. We house a total of 2,800 individual primates, not including the staff."

"You sound like you've given this spiel before."

"Many times. That rock formation on your right is eighty-four feet high and tall as a four-story building. It's an exact replica of a cliff face in Tanzania, where some of our first animals were taken. On the far right, that gray slab jutting out? The large male beside the log is named Morgan. Sort of the patriarch of the clan. That pile of leaves is where he's been nesting for three or four nights, which they asked me to mention because he's never removed himself from the others this far before. It's probably Morgan on camera making a threat gesture just before the incident."

"Threat gesture?"

"Their hackles go up, and they yawn. Chimps've got a set of fangs like Count Dracula."

"I didn't see any bite marks on the body."

"They'll clobber the shit out of you too. And throw stuff. Your average chimp is a lot stronger than an adult human. And their temperament doesn't improve with age."

"You saying the husband did it?"

"I'm saying you've handled more of these than I have."

"So. How serious are your protesters?

"Depends. We have several species of those—the no-fur crowd, PETA, Animal Liberation Front, Earth Firsters. Every once in a while a few of them will get past security and trash a lab or spring a few animals."

"And it might look bad for the Center if the wrong kind of story got out. Hold up the research and all that."

"Yeah. You're catching on."

"Bad enough to close you down?"

"I doubt it. The stakes are too high. This is the last stop before major medical trials on humans, and we're talking about pharmaceuticals, implants, tissue cultures, and new operative procedures. There's money going through here like coke through Colombia."

"Great. So this Deckard. He's really onto something big?"

"We believe so."

"Okay. How about I talk to this other chimp, the one named Morgan?"

"Talk to him?"

"Yeah. He can do sign language, right?"

"You want to interview a chimp?"

"You said go anywhere I want, ask anything I want. So why not ask the guy who was there?"

"I'll see what I can do. But we've got less than twenty-two hours, and I've got a hell of a lot of writing to do. How about we review the tape first."

"How about I talk to the chimp first."

"I'll see what I can do."

The caretaker brought him on a leash. Morgan himself closed the door but stiffened when he saw Stillman sitting beneath the mirror on the far side of the room. "It's okay," the caretaker said. "Here, let me take this off. Now hop on your box. Hop up here the way we always do."

Morgan clambered onto a carpet-covered box and scooped up the grape on his side of the table, holding it between his lip and gum for a moment, taking it out of his mouth for a closer look, and then popping it back in for a satisfying chew. He glared at Stillman and then at the keyboard on his side of the table. He raised one arm and jabbed twice at the oversized pictograms like a man with a mechanical hand. On the computer screen next to Stillman a word and an image appeared. *Grape.* When the woman caretaker did not respond, he tried more keys. The first screen cleared, to be replaced by *Juice. More. Juice.*

Stillman watched from the low chair at the end of the table.

The woman was bent over her duffel bag, drawing out toys, cups, bottles, and recording paraphernalia.

Morgan rocked back and forth on his box, stretching his lips into a wide grimace, and then typed again. *Sylvia. Juice. Sylvia. Juice. Cup.*

"I think he wants some juice," said Stillman.

"I know. And you don't have to whisper. He's used to the routine. Just let me finish here. You can give him half a cup."

Stillman poured orange juice into one of the tiny paper cups, the kind he'd seen in nursery schools, and set it on the table in front of the creature. Morgan leaned forward and sniffed before lifting the cup with delicate care and setting it in the palm of his left hand. Then, making a funnel with his mouth, he raised the cup further and poured.

"You have to take it away from him," she continued, "or he'll scrape off the wax with his teeth and eat it."

When Stillman reached, the animal hunched his shoulders and glared, crumpling the cup against his stomach.

"I don't think he's going to give it up."

"Oh, for heaven's sake, just wait a minute, both of you. Let me turn down the lights and get the recorder going. Here, give me that." She plucked the cup from the thick fingers and put it into a plastic bag. To Stillman she said, "Just stay where you are and don't lurch around. He's a little uncomfortable. A grin like that could be a threat, but more likely it's just nervousness."

"Let's get this over with."

"Okay, let me just ask him a few preliminary questions." Sylvia the caretaker placed a ball on the table and touched one of the keys on the console. The screen showed a question mark in the pictogram box and the word *What?* To the right of the box.

The crooked finger went automatically to a red key while the eyes remained unnervingly on Stillman. *Ball* said the screen.

Sylvia took the ball away and gave Morgan another grape, which he took between cheek and gum while he watched for the next object, an empty paper cup. Without waiting for the question, the chimp hit another key. *Cup.*

"Good!" She reached across the table and scratched one ear and patted the head.

Juice. Grape. Cup flashed the screen.

Without looking at Stillman the woman said, "This is one of the reasons that chimps in general are such great subjects. They're greedy. They'll steal food right out of your pocket."

"Let's just ask him what I wrote out for you. I'm getting a little claustrophobic."

"You'll have to be patient. You can't just skip ahead to a complicated concept. In fact, one of the big questions is whether they understand syntax at all. You get garbled answers if you push them too hard."

"How come he keeps looking at me like that?"

"Just be still. He's nervous. I've got to take him through some verbs first."

After a few more exchanges, the caretaker finally looked down at Stillman's notes and typed. *Question. Who. Hurt. Greta. Question.*
Ball. Greta.

"What's wrong? Why didn't he answer?"

"Maybe he doesn't know. Maybe we're asking the wrong question. Or asking the right question the wrong way. It often takes several tries. *Question. Greta. Hurt. Question.*
Yes.

Who?

Big. Ball.

Question. What. Hurt. Greta. Question.

Big. Light.

Question. Who. Question. Who. Hurt. Greta. Question.

Greta.

Who?

Greta. Juice. Grape.

Question. Greta. Big. Hurt. Question?

Yes.

Question. Who. Question.

Grape.

Who?

More. Banana. Light.

"I don't know," said Stillman. "I don't think this is working. He doesn't know what planet he's on."

"I'm sorry," said the caretaker. "Maybe if you gave him just a few more minutes."

"Yeah, well . . . maybe he'd be more comfortable if it was just the two of you. Thanks anyhow." Stillman eased past them and into the heavy atmosphere of the compound, then used a pass card to open the door into the corridor. He patted his coat pockets for a cigarette and noticed a quiet figure standing next to the two-way observation mirror. It was Deckard.

After a moment he turned to the detective and said, "That was ingenious, Mr. Stillman. I would never have thought simply to ask."

"It was worth a try."

"Did you learn anything?"

"Yeah, should have gone to the tape first."

I sat Stillman down at the computer and called up the media player. Then clicked play. The images on-screen began with a stuttering burst of light, like film skipping in an old-fashioned projector. In all, the sequence lasted sixty-three seconds. Stillman watched the events cycle four or five times, gradually leaning left as if he could pick up action that had occurred off camera. I watched him studying the moment of Greta's death and wondered how many humans he'd seen die from this same perspective, images from ceiling cameras in pawn shops and convenience stores.

At 0224.14 on the blinking timeline, a hunched shape backed into the frame, then immediately charged forward out of range, reappearing again at 0224.33. I told him it was Greta. He could see the rest. Her hackles were raised and lips drawn back in a rictus of fear. She shook her head like a wet dog. Then another whiteout obscured a stamping display, and a second figure emerged from the emptiness at the left of the screen. I told him it was Morgan, also clearly agitated. He looked like a furious old man shaking his head no, no, no, no. Then at 0225.16 Greta turned toward the camera, a mask of insane terror frozen on her face; and she threw herself at the edge of the cliff. That was all. She was gone in less than a second.

"Let's see it again," said Stillman.

I showed him how to work the media player. He clicked with the mouse and once more watched Greta backing into the last moments of her life. "And there's no sound at all?"

"Nope. And no artificial lighting inside the compound. When it's dark outside, it's dark in the compound."

"Then what are those flashes of light?"

"Beats me. Maybe heat lightning."

"And what about that?"

"Right there? Looks like an edge of the steel framing that holds up the roof, you know, one of the sections of the dome."

"No way to enlarge any of this?"

"You could, but the resolution would be worse. What are you looking for?"

"I don't know."

He started the sequence again. And again it was night. There was the lightninglike burst of whiteness and then a sweeping shot of the rock ledge. In the upper third of the frame, through the clear dome of their world, wheeled the slow stars of the Milky Way. And in the foreground were the rocks that we call the escarpment. Creeping into the lower left were the uppermost branches of massasa and mahogany. At 0224.14 Stillman's muppet backed into the scene as before and mustered enough desperation to charge on all fours. Then stayed out of view for nineteen seconds. Then the second lightning flash revealed Morgan, shaking his head and flailing a branch that he had broken at some lower elevation and dragged with him to the peak. And then there was something else that caught Stillman's attention as the terrified chimp slapped, open handed, at her own eyes. Just before she turned and launched herself into the void.

"Right there," he said. "What's that?"

"I don't see anything."

"Looks like a shoe."

"Might be a shadow."

"It might be a shoe."

"I'm not saying you're wrong. I'm just . . ."

"I think it's time to get that magnification now."

"Maybe it's time to talk. Let's step out in the hall for a second." Which is when I told him the truth. He would have figured it out in another hour. Besides, the truth wasn't relevant. It hardly ever is.

"You know why I picked you?"

"I just assumed it was a combination of the swimsuit and talent competitions."

"I picked you because I thought you might understand if it ever got this far."

"Meaning what exactly?"

"Meaning that we can do things, right now, that we couldn't do even a year ago. Meaning that these people, Stillman, are on the verge of curing half a dozen diseases, perfecting noninvasive surgery, regenerating nerves, you name it."

"And you thought what, that you could put my name on the list if they ever whipped up a cure for deafness?"

"No."

"Then what?"

"ALS is a funny disease. You can never predict which neurons in the brain and spinal cord it'll attack. Sometimes it paralyzes the arms and legs. Sometimes it affects speech or breathing first. They say Lou Gehrig himself eventually choked to death. There's no cure, no therapy, and nothing on the immediate horizon except for the slight possibility that the man you met this morning really is a genius. And that I can get Janie into the first human trials. Right now she's having trouble swallowing, and I figure in a few months it won't make any difference whether the human trials are approved or not. That's what I was hoping you could understand."

For a long time Stillman said nothing. He wiped at his face with both hands as if trying to wash away the fatigue, then sat on one of the low benches that lined the hall.

So I pressed him some more. "The procedure works. We already know that. The problem was that Greta showed some anomalies, not enough to wreck the experiment, but enough to throw off the data. So we had to start reverification. Fast. All we're asking you to do is sign a piece of paper, so we can start over with a clean slate."

"How did you do it?" he said.

"Strobe light. You know, from the break-in at the photo lab. We figured if worse came to worst, we could blame it on some protesters."

"'We' meaning you and Dr. Deckard."

"It was his idea actually. After the procedure she'd had, it would overload her brain. She'd do anything to get away from it."

"So you made a deal. Deckard gets something he wants. You get something you want. The only person hurt is a monkey. Let me ask you something, chief. Do you trust the guy that much?"

"Do I have a choice?"

Maybe I should have told him that it was all an insurance scam. It would have been easier. That's what he believed at first, and maybe he would have gone for the money. You can never tell. Even if you're spinning the absolute truth, you can never tell what kind of lies people will believe. Especially old cops. Now he would have to decide. And I'm not sure I could have chosen correctly myself. At five o'clock it was still raining the way it had been earlier, and I drove him back to his office after telling him I would e-mail a copy of his report tomorrow morning. And that Peggy could print it on their letterhead and fax it back to me in the afternoon, after he'd signed it. If that's what he felt he could do.

On the way downtown he asked me when I thought they could start human trials.

I said a few weeks, maybe a couple of months, if we stayed on the fast track.

He looked at me like he thought I'd believe anything.

The rest of the drive was silent. I let him out in the scabby parking lot of his office, and he went inside after a slight wave of the hand. I watched him flick on the overhead lights and head down the hall toward one of the cubicles.

Then I pulled back into the deserted street and followed the yellow line.

Back at the Center I headed toward my own office to begin work on the incident report. I needed to finish it and also a press release about a new cholesterol drug being developed jointly by us and a major pharmaceutical company. It would take a couple of hours, but both items needed to go out the next day. First, though, I called home and got Janie on the speakerphone. Told her that I'd be late and that I'd get Mrs. Carrillo to come over and stay the night. She wasn't happy, but she understood the job, and its benefits, better than I did. So I hung up and went by the cafeteria for coffee and a sandwich, the way I used to do when I was a reporter. Banging away on a story that would be old news by morning.

Then I took the elevator up, balancing coffee in one hand and briefcase and sandwich in the other. Sipping gingerly. Hoping Stillman would come around after he dismounted from his high horse. Taking the glassed-in hallway, the syringe, that connected the two wings of the medical section. Halfway across, almost precisely where I had stopped Stillman earlier in the day, I met a lab assistant pushing a gurney like the ones in hospitals. I had to step aside and to control the momentary horror of stepping into an abyss.

Strapped to the gurney was my friend Morgan, partially sedated and on his way to the Emerald City where Deckard and the others waited for him. He seemed neither frightened nor enraged by his restraints but merely puzzled. His face looked like a sleepy child's. And he wore a disposable diaper, already urine soaked and limp around his waist. His eyes seemed drawn to the car headlights in the parking lot far below, but as we passed he looked in my direction and seemed to find something that he recognized. He made a slight movement with one of his hands, perhaps an attempt to communicate in sign language, who could know? Maybe it was only a reflex.

The next morning I asked Sylvia the caregiver to bring me one of those little charts they use to teach sign language to the chimps, and on it I looked in vain for the word he had left in the air. For days I wondered if he had been reaching for some unprinted thing, or only a circus word. Like *grape* or *juice* or *cup*.

THEY HAVE REPLACEABLE
VALVES AND FILTERS

The Cave

FOR SUSAN

In my mind I see the six of them hunched in the shade like a chain gang, exhausted, their fingers cut and caked with mud, faces already gone blank with despair. I imagine Burke down on his haunches, wrists hung over his knees, with a cigarette maybe, studying that ragged hole like it was his own grave. Their daddy, name of Lucas Bender, standing off by himself. And one of the twins praying, or maybe just hoping out loud, I don't know. You can imagine that second day at the cave any way you want. It don't change a thing.

I expect one of them finally said, "We could try and get that wild girl lives over to Flint Ridge. She might could crawl under the outcrop, reach him some food and a blanket so he don't freeze. I mean, if we could find her."

Which they did.

Plucked me out of a chinaberry tree. Carried me over the tourist road in a Model T Ford, my first ever ride in an automobile, to a no-name holler where the world had caved in on Lee Bender, and there I was. A whole new place. The same mountain blue sky as my sky, yes. And the same cotton white clouds, same layer on layer of greenness all tumbling over the crest of the mountain and down to towns where girls my age didn't wear overalls or bob their hair or ride off with strangers. But hill folk are different; and here I was not even surprised at a man who looked like Moses stepping me down from the running board of that Model T, saying, "Lucas Bender. This'd be Burke, Asa, Ronnie, and Donnie that brung you, and Hugh. I knew your granddaddy. And we obliged to you." Like he had all the time in the world.

That's what I remember of my life before the cave.

My childhood came and went. Like a long courtship, with wildflowers, honeycakes for breakfast, running, running, running along ledges only one step away from clouds, like you could just throw yourself out and they would catch you in the quilting of it. That's what I recall. Then the little heart shapes of sun and shadow flickering over his face. So handsome. And Burke a gentle, lumbering man who's standing in the creek to his knees, offering to carry me over like a town girl; but I jump, scramble up the bank without slipping once, and find the opening on my own right next to a mountain laurel. Because I've been in woods and caves all my life.

When I grab the branch, pink petals come twirling like snowflakes, and he's quietly behind me saying, "That air blowing in your face, it found its way from underground." He knows that he must stay calm and quiet because I might startle like a colt and then their trip would have been in vain. So Burke's voice is sleepy and slow, light enough that it nearly floats away. "What they call a breathing cave. My brother's trapped down there, but it ain't like you imagine. It won't be like climbing down into no grave, Rachel Ann, and I won't let nothing smother you. It'll breathe out like this for fifteen, twenty minutes, then, after a spell, breathe in. You can feel it the whole time. I seen it suck in a dragonfly this morning and then let it back out not even wrinkling the wings."

"It's cold," I say.

"It's fresh and clean too, like running water."

"It's cold as the grave, and there's a man down there, ain't that right?"

"It's constant fifty-one degrees," he says. "Lee told me hisself. Same temperature year-round. Fifty-one in July. Fifty-one in January."

"Either way you could die."

"It ain't like you imagine," he insists. "Nothing ever is."

And talks me in by degrees. He carries the blanket and the lantern. I take the paper sack and the longbar from the Model T's toolbox. Near the entrance it's sand and gravel like a railroad tunnel, then shale farther back, and finally smooth limestone sloping off in three directions. Burke picks the middle passage that still gets some light from the entrance, but pretty soon he's bending over and shuffling like an old man, and in another minute he is crawling. Then, after a while, I am crawling too. Just scrunching and twisting for years until it's not fun at all and my hands begin to look like theirs, my elbows raw, and I am not fourteen years old, and I am not a mountain girl anymore. Until he finally stops, saying, "Why don't you scoot on past me while I light the lantern."

And for a moment we are like man and wife.

In the yellow kerosene light I can see the outcropping that's blocked their way and the dirt piles where they've tried to dig around it, but there is no hole, only dust and leavings. Because I am little, I can still sit with my back against the wall and see Burke, who's struggling on his side now, shoulders almost touching floor and ceiling at the same time. He's panting when he puts his face down low into the dirt and shouts under the outcropping, "Lee! Lee, we brung somebody. Gonna pry you loose. Got a blanket for you. Can you hear me? Lee! It's me Burke."

But there is no answer, only a blank black oval underneath the outcropping where you would never think to look. After two days of patient chipping they have made it twelve inches wide. I can feel the sharp-toothed edges with my hand, and suddenly I cannot breathe for thinking about it. I cannot move at all. My mind wants to run away into another place, but I can still feel his hands on my hips, even today, right now, his lover's caress and patient insistence, and then I am through.

I go tumbling down, down like rotten tree limbs under a load of snow, at first only sagging over the edge and then crashing down through rocks and slippery soil until I collide with the very thing that I have imagined. It is soft and wet and full of frightening strength, the hands crawling over my face as I gasp and fight. I'm touching him in a different place every time I push away, and we are tangled together until finally I can relax and back away upslope, while he moans.

"I got him," I whisper to the cave, "I did it, I'm through, I got him," water dripping into water somewhere in the darkness. I'm shaking with cold and fear and effort, shouting, "I got him!" back toward his brother on the other side. The words come out in a jumble, get caught on an inrushing current, and echo. "Pass me that sack, no, the blanket. No. Wait. Pass me that lantern first."

It comes through sideways, and I have to relight, but I am slow and steady now. This is not my first cave, my first corpse. It's not my first dark night of day, because I am a mountain girl. I know sunshine and storms. Both my mamma and daddy by the age of nine. And now Lee Bender who is fish-belly white, caught between two boulders. A weak and wasted version of his brother on the other side, he squints and twists away from the light that burns right through the crook of his arm and sets fire to his brain; and I know in that first glance that Lee Bender will die because he has become a part of the cave. I turn the lantern low out of pity. Then from out the shadow his dry voice is rasping, "Who is it?"

And I'm yelling back, "He's okay! He's moving around some."

"Who are you?" Like I am a ghost.

"Rachel Ann Starns from over about Flint Ridge. I come to give you this." And hand him the paper sack.

Lee Bender's arms are free. They are long and thin like spider legs and come dribbling dust so fine that it glistens, slowly, slowly, until he can reach up to where I am reaching down. He takes the sack but cannot unroll the top and tears it open the way a crayfish would tear. And picks at the pieces. Inside it is a crust of cornbread, which he crumbles and lifts to his mouth with fingers gone straight and stiff with cold. And there is a jar half full of buttermilk, which he takes in sips. "You don't know how thankful I am for this, Rachel Ann Starns. God's gonna bless you real good."

"He's eating it!" I yell back, and then scramble up to take the blanket that Burke has passed through the hole.

But even the good you do.

It makes me cry sometimes. There is loose rock all around, and I have kicked down several big ones, sent sand and gravel sliding, and buried him to his chest. I've made his mouth go small and round, gulping at the air like a fish flopping, but it's done with such slow finality that it takes my breath even now. And I am paralyzed again. But it is what happens in a cave. You are caught. Through the billowing dust you see him pull one arm out of the muck, patiently digging the other one loose handful by handful. You watch as he starts picking away the rocks one by one, delicately, dropping them away into the darkness where they give back no sound at all.

From far away I can hear the trapped man saying, "It ain't the boulders holding me. It ain't the riprap. They's just one tiny little rock. Broke off when I was climbing out this crawl space and must have fell just right. Cause when I jerked my leg—," he pauses, almost embarrassed I believe, "—hit just clicked into place. Like the closing of a door. It don't even hurt."

So I cover his shoulders with the blanket and brush the filth from his hair and caress his forehead to take away the pain because I already know there is that much in the touch of a woman's hand.

Then just before Burke pulls me through, his brother comes alive to me, saying, "Don't worry, Rachel Ann Starns. You an angel of God. This ain't such a bad place, you know that now. Tell 'em. With this blanket, little food, Lee Bender can stay down here a month if he has to. I'm not in any pain. You tell 'em that. Tell my brothers I'm not in any pain, just a mite uncomfortable. I been a caver all my life. Been stuck before too. My brothers'll get me out and my daddy, and, besides, lift up your eyes and look."

I have already passed through the lantern, but we no longer need the light. I see it hovering over me, as clear as a cloud against a mountain sky, glistening white, as ripply smooth as melted wax. At the top it curves into a half circle, all the rest just flowing away to one side and down so that it looks like a lace window curtain blown sideways in a breeze. You would never think anything made in stone could be this delicate. All along, left to right, it just drips away in creamy folds that have the overlapping delicacy of feathers. "Like an angel's wing," I say.

"That's what it is," whispers Lee Bender. Laying his head down on the blanket that I had brought him and closing his eyes in sleep.

Outside, the holler has changed.

I don't know how they got there so fast. It may have been a telephone somewhere, or the cars. But like magic they are there, twenty or thirty of them when we come out. Helpers helping us down the embankment. Women with baskets of food. Men, relatives I reckon, with their sleeves rolled up, coats hanging from tree limbs. Silent sad-eyed children among the galax and ferns. They are all staring at us like we just clawed our way up from another world. And I am staring back at them in the hush of it all, not realizing that I have taken his hand, and someone behind us is murmuring, like in a dream, "I thought you said hit was a girl."

And there is a flatbed truck now piled with wheelbarrows, rope, shovels, picks. A man handing them down one at a time. I can see where they've brought it down the holler, a green furrow of branches and saplings all bent in the same direction like a fish trap. Straddling the creek. Backed up to the opening as near as they could get it. And farther upstream, between the ruts, men are harnessing two mules, tying heavy ropes to the traces like they come to pull stumps. And somebody is trying to shush a pack of hounds that think it's time to hunt.

Burke speaks to his daddy in low urgent tones. "She done good. Got through and all. Next thing is maybe get some fellas in there with cold chisels, widen that hole."

He nods, fumbling with his pocket watch. "I don't know," he says. "I don't know what's next to do. I just want him outta there." Then closes the cover with a snap, like he could stop time if he clicked fast enough and buried it deep enough in his pocket. But it is on a chain, and the chain is hooked to his overalls.

Across the creek in a ragged clearing is a man whose voice draws stragglers in ones and twos. It is a child's voice, tinny and distant, and it is a child's body except for the face, where time and pain have done their work. He stands upon a stump, both arms raised to the sky, both hands clamped upon a ragged black book, piping in that high radio voice, "You know, Lord God, that this world is rotton and corrup'. Undergirt with treachery. And that the earth that abideth forever will claim any who will not lift up their eyes, amen. Surely and purely it is set forth as a sign among us, and so we pray this afternoon for your fallen servant Lee, ask that you smite the rock and stay the hand and restore him once again to the love a his family, amen. Bring forth a miracle as in the days of our Lord and Savior Jesus Christ, amen."

"What's going on here?" says Burke.

"Name of Reverent Josephus Harwell," says Asa. "He come with Thomas and Louisa, I reckon. Took up in that clearing as soon's he got here midafternoon. Been gospel slinging ever since. Say one time he was with the carnival till he got saved."

"He ain't no bigger'n her. Whyn't you send him down?"

The wind smothers the answer, driving the preacher's words higher and whipping his hair to one side till his words come back to earth as a chant. "They ain't nobody here can take a man out of the ground nor loose the grip a Satan. They's only one way to get lifted up, and we going to pray for Lee Bender and Brother Lucas and his family, yes we are, until there's enough God in this holler to split open the earth and lay a golden staircase all the way down to that poor boy. We gonna bless every man that goes into that hillside, every shovel, pickax, every inch of rope, every woman that brung food, every neighbor who brung hope. We gonna bless every mule and wagon that comes down that road and every free breath of air we take. Because why? Because the earth under our feet is a empty shell, amen."

"Fine," Burke manages. "Just pray it don't rain first. And that you can find me two men with hammers and chisels."

"We can't have that kind of talk, Burke." Lucas seems like a man who's come back from a far place. "I don't care how tired and wore out you are."

"Look, it ain't the devil that's got hold of him. It's a rock. That's all."

After a time they made a half circle before the stump, and a few of the men who'd been unloading tools drifted across the creek and took up with the women and children. Someone began a low moaning of a tune that followed exactly the preacher's incantation. A family just arriving went straight to the gathering without even looking once toward the cave. And after a time Lucas Bender and the twins crossed the creek and sat, hands folded in desperate prayer.

We stay behind.

Burke says again, "You done good an' I thank you. I don't reckon we can get you home before dark, but you welcome to stay with one of the families. People say you practically live in the woods anyhow."

"I live with my aunts."

"You don't live in the woods with the animals?"

"I been to school."

"I been to school too," he says, "but they didn't teach climbing and caving when I went."

"I can read. I know the medieval ages, the Bible, and the Roman empire. I can sew and cook and—"

"I don't mean nothing by it, Rachel Ann Starns. You done good. One of these days . . . , why, one of these days, I'm gonna bring you flowers. Right now I'm just tired. That's all." He hands me his pocket-knife. "Here. S'all I have that's worth anything. Why don't you whittle us up a house, some furniture. Some supper." Then he collapses on the fern bank, propping himself on one elbow and taking short sips from a mason jar that he passes back and forth with a fat, unshaven man who guards his basket with suspicious care. After a time Burke closes his eyes like he's listening to music and says, "Whatta you reckon, Solly?"

The bootlegger scratches his stubble. "I think maybe this is the last place on earth that God ain't got around to yet. What's your brother doing out here anyhow?"

Burke opens his eyes long enough to point and then closes them again. "Eight miles down that road is the entrance to Mammoth Cave. Like a tourist gold mine is what it is, and eight miles closer to town than we are here."

"Caving's big business. People'll pay to see another world."

"Yeah, well, another mile or so out this way is the Morrison entrance to Mammoth Cave. Big signs everywhere, souvenirs. They do right well. Then Sells Store a little farther out. Then Great Onyx Cave, where they got a hotel now. Then Crystal Cave. Then Crystal Lake. More souvenir places, campgrounds."

"I see what you mean."

"Cause you know where we are right now, Solly? We at the shag end of a muddy, spring-busting road. But my brother Lee, he believes people would come if he could just find something spectacular enough, and we wouldn't be at the end of the road no more."

"You'd need a miracle sure enough."

"When me and Lee were boys, we'd tramp through the fields in winter till we found a sinkhole, sometimes right out in the middle of a cornfield. And we found out you could flop down on the ground and blow down into one of them, and pretty soon you could see your own breath come floating back out. To him that was a miracle, a sign that the world was alive all around you. I guess he never stopped looking."

The man named Solly takes a pull from his jar and gestures at the congregation. "I lived here all my life. I don't even know that preacher man's name, I never seen him before. Makes you wonder where he was last summer when there was no rain, don't it?"

"All I know is—I'm going back down. You coming with me?"

But the fat man must have thought that Burke was talking to me. And my next trip into Sand Cave lasted for years.

Sometimes even today I go back. Where I can see it all so clearly. I think to myself. I think, girl, why do you go back into that place? What is it that you hope to find when you go back to a place for the second time? And then I remember. I say, why, it's all the things you didn't see before because not even a cave is absolute darkness. There are miracles all around you.

I see white crystal chandeliers sparkling in a ballroom where even girls in overalls can dance.

I see the princess room, with her very own pallet spread over the floor and her pillows all covered with cloth of gold. Chairs and tables of swirled marble and fountains bubbling with water so pure and cold you could take one drink and know you were in a fairy tale. And from her window you could look down into a garden where glass flowers blossom and glimmer vines go curling out like clay squeezed through your fingers.

I walk through deserted temples that look like ruins from the *Geographic*, columns so tall they stretch up to nothing. A staircase as clear as melted glass. And I know I am the only girl from Flint Ridge to hear the pipe organ as wind goes whirling through the cathedral and lifts my hair. I chime out notes on pipes that double themselves in quiet water. And once, after we talk to him again, we find Lee's meadow, the secret winter world where crystal snow has fallen in perfect flakes and just your breath will drop whole trees to powder.

We make him as comfortable as we can. Tell him that help is on the way. I try to reach his ankle that is caught, but it's no use. We move bushels of rock and dirt, make a pillow of his brother's coat, feed him bread and cheese, dig down past his waist, but it's no use. We stay with Lee Bender until he is an old man too feeble to struggle anymore.

Then stumble back out to a world that had changed itself again. Filled with strangers and no one calls our name. Smoke and surge of a gasoline generator drowning out words, throwing off electricity for the strings of lightbulbs all flung through the trees. So that at first I do not even realize it is night.

We walk past a line of men waiting for orders, fidgeting with their tools while a colonel from the Army Corps of Engineers studies his map laid out on a wooden table, arguing with men wearing wrinkled ties, suspenders over sweat-stained shirts. As if during a summer night's dream our little holler had grown into a town.

"Where's daddy?" Burke is saying. "What's going on here?" He takes a passing man by the shoulder when no one answers. "Hey, listen to me, where's my brother Asa?"

"You the one been down there all this time? Your brother done left. Him and the colonel had a falling out. But you might better see to your daddy first. He don't look too good, just drifted off to the edge of things after the governor—"

"The governor?"

"Your name Burke, ain't it?"

"What if it is?"

"Lissen, Burke, you been down a long time. This here story's out over the radio, in all the newspapers. They's reporters here now. Volunteers from Illinois and Pennsylvania, miners, I reckon. They thinking about sinking another shaft if we can't winch him out."

And below the embankment I can see a length of cable being wound onto a big metal spool, two men cranking backwards while two more feed the line. Burke stumbles away into the crowd while I look at silhouettes, listen to the hubbub of the town that has found us. Once I think I see Lucas in the shadows, but it could have been any bent-over old man; it is just a shape. And so is Reverend Harwell, who has his own bonfire now and a dressed-up congregation seated in fold-up chairs. A shape and a sound against the flickering light. I make it up to the main road and walk between a double row of Model Ts leaning into the ditches on both sides. Past a wooden pushcart where a man is selling cider and sandwiches. On out along the ridge until I can't hear the harmonica player or the low rumble of machinery.

Three days is how long it takes. After that it is a carnival. Bootleggers sneaking down into the work tents. Picture takers gathering up whole families and posing them near the entrance. A woman who sells balloons saying SAND CAVE. A radio reporter who crawls his microphone underground and broadcasts the victim's low breathing now that he has lost consciousness.

I sit on a trunk and talk to a newspaperman who writes fast in his notebook. Was he still alive when I last went in? What did he say? Does he know that the whole country is listening, that he is famous? How does he feel? Some folks think he is already dead, that all this is just wasted effort. Some think he really isn't trapped at all, that he leaves by a back entrance and sleeps in his own bed at night.

"What are you saying?" I stammer.

The reporter tilts his hat back a bit. "I'm just saying they might be people who think this is all a hoax. All done up for show. I mean you being the only one who's actually talked to him—that right? How old are you, missy? What grade are you in?"

"Leave her alone," says Burke Bender.

They send in a jack to pry apart the boulders. It slips away. They send in a doctor to amputate the leg. He can't reach into the crawlway. They send in a pneumatic drill to cut the hole wider. Part of the ceiling collapses. And they start digging the second shaft. Nobody knows what to do.

Finally they give me a leather harness attached to a rope. "See if you can work this past the squeezeway," says the colonel. "Get the harness on him, and we'll just do whatever it takes. He's too weak to last much longer; we got to get him out no matter what."

"How do you mean?" I say.

"Just pull. Pull his leg off if we have to."

And I go in for the third time.

The microphone is halfway down the first corridor. They must have run out of wire; it's not even close to the outcropping. Farther back are bottles of milk, sandwiches, blankets that have been piled up on the near side of the hole, a scattering of burned-out lanterns just within the first darkness; but I wiggle through to him with no trouble.

"It's Rachel Ann," I say.

"What year is it?" comes a frail voice.

"It's July third. Nineteen and twenty-six. They's people all over the place up there. They writing about you in the newspapers."

"Where's Burke?"

"It's just me now. I brought a rope. They want to hitch you up, pull you out."

"Pass it down. I need to go home now, Rachel Ann. I can't feel my legs anymore."

"Can you get in the harness?"

"I'm in."

"Okay," I yell back. "Take it slow."

They pull for twenty minutes, at the end adding more and more power until I think the rope will break under the weight of his cries. Once he passes out and then finally comes awake enough to sob, "Stop. For the love of God, stop! I'd rather die where I am than—"

And I cut the rope.

No one knows how long. It takes a week to dig the second shaft, a full day to get a doctor down, two more to cut away the stone that held his foot. And by then no one cares to lift the body out. It is Burke who finally does it. They enlarge the entrance to the place now called officially Sand Cave, embalm his body, and lay it in a casket forty feet back beneath a painted sign. "HERE LIE THE MORTAL REMAINS OF JAMES LEE BENDER. AUGUST 12, 1898–JULY 5, 1926. THE WORLD'S GREATEST CAVE EXPLORER." And people come for years.

My hands are cracked and caked with mud when I emerge. I feel so tired and frail, and the young doctor is saying, "How's my girl, how are we feeling today? Let me just have a listen, can you cough for me? Again. Okay. Now cough again. That's fine. Are the eyedrops working?"

"I'm cold," I say.

"We'll get you a blanket. It's the air-conditioning. I'll have one of the nurses bring you a blanket. Are you eating okay?"

"I like a mite of salt on my vegetables. You people ever heard of salt?"

But, no, he doesn't hear me. He asks if I would like a stroll this afternoon, would I like Raymond to roll me out to the courtyard, get some sunshine, would that be nice?

"I want to go home," I say.

"Mrs. Bender, we've talked about that. Do you remember?"

"No."

"Well, I have a surprise for you. There's a young man who wants very much to see you. He's waiting out at the nurse's station. I'm going to send him in as soon as we take a little blood sample."

And then he is here in the room with me. So tall and straight, so handsome when he hugs my neck that I can see from all those years ago. I know the voice. It says, "Hey, Grandma. It's me, Burke. I brought you flowers."

"I know who you are. You're one of my babies."

"How are they treating you, Grandma? Are you okay?"

I have to pat his hand. I pat. And that's all it takes. The tremor drops away from his voice, and after a time the shoulders relax inside the leather jacket, and we are talking like old friends through the afternoon. He rolls me, bump-bump, out onto the patio where the sunlight and birds are. And the blue mountain shapes in the distance. I try to tell him don't be afraid. But we hear some old woman instead. I try to say don't be afraid, it's not like you imagine. But she's interrupting, spilling the words everywhere. "When I was a girl," she says. "When I was a girl. I was wild and free."

Here's a Shot of Us at the Grand Canyon

FOR MATT

In fact they can be located quite precisely. The satellite photograph in infrared shows a set of curves and cantilevers upon a wooded lot at the end of a cul-de-sac within a gated community inside of a small town on the edge of a city. It is an image of their house. The splotches are heat sources, perhaps individuals, perhaps poorly insulated appliances. Who can say?

Outside there is a narrow band of fescue, no wider than a moat, holding off the wilderness, and during the summer Roger hacks at tendrils of poison ivy as if they were tentacles reaching up from unimaginable depths. Amy watches through a perfectly round portal. He rakes, mows, and grooms an impeccable houndstooth of needles at the edge of the woods. She brushes her hair straight back, pulling tightly enough to lift the furrows from her face and create an epicanthic fold. Yet she never blinks.

It is a haunted house.

Amy and Roger have a pale white son named Wesley, perhaps a piano prodigy, who plays Chopin at age nine with incredible speed and efficiency, his nimble fingers more expressive than his face. It is the same way he plays Nintendo, all grace and fury within the machine, so that when they call him down for dinner on most nights, he flicks the joystick, presses the button for a spinning jump, and replies tonelessly, "I'm coming. Just let me kill myself first."

They worry, of course. These are not heartless people. They are not stupid and insensitive.

They want Wesley to be like other children at Stolpen Country Day but not like other children too. It's all very complex.

Their therapist, Dr. Rohmer, is a soft and maternal woman who looks like Mrs. Dilettuso, the cleaning lady. "He's quite intelligent," the doctor acknowledges. "His mental development is actually far beyond . . ."

"We already know that," Roger interrupts. "I'm sorry, but we already know that. What should we be *doing*?"

Because she never hurries an answer, the therapist has time to gather herself and then almost smiles. "Nothing out of the ordinary. He's a little boy. I would suggest doing little boy things with him."

"That's your diagnosis? We're paying a small fortune, enough to have made him a full boarder at Benfield, and that's your recommendation? A play group?" Amy is nervous and disappointed.

And so Dr. Rohmer searches for a word she can give them, a name for the thing without a name, hoping that they can begin to heal as soon as they can identify the disease. She thinks through several texts and finally says, "I suspect a condition called *alexythemia*. It means 'without words for feelings.'"

Roger bristles. "You're suggesting that our son is retarded?"

"Not at all. These people are often quite intelligent. And they do have emotions."

"What do you mean they 'do have' emotions?"

Already Dr. Rohmer regrets taking this path. She realizes that it's not what they need to hear, but now there's no turning back. She crosses her legs and makes a note on her notepad. "Alexythemics can distinguish between 'good' and 'bad' experiences; they just can't attach language to what they're feeling. It's a condition—not a disease—that affects perhaps five percent of the population. The subjects are over-whelmingly male."

"You're saying that I gave birth to a sadist?"

"No. No, this is difficult to grasp, I realize, and I'm certainly not an expert. What I'm suggesting is that someone with this particular disorder cannot distinguish between, for instance, fear and sadness. Or anger, for that matter. He could tell you that these feelings are all 'bad' in some sense—but that might be the extent of his discrimina-tion."

"So it's a disorder now?"

"That's crazy," muses Roger.

"I've got the name of someone I could give you. A specialist if that would make you feel better."

"A specialist? What would we do in the meantime?"

"Nothing extraordinary. Little boy things, like playing outside. You might consider getting a pet, a dog maybe."

"Oh God."

"Is something the matter?"

"It's such a cliché," Amy moans.

In any case, it is a big house, an expensive heap of white stucco and glass thrown up in the Mediterranean style. A house of many lev-els. The interior has been professionally decorated, the furnishings contemporary and severe. Some of the walls meet at acute angles and some simply stop, but there are plants to soften sharp corners: ficus and fern on green marble pedestals, African violets, arrange-ments of silk flowers. It looks like the architectural drawing of a house, a model set down for inspection in the architect's studio. But there are many humanizing effects. It is a lived-in house with fabric wall hangings, shelves of authentic tribal artifacts from areas of the world where savagery has become fashionable once again. Books. Magazines. A baby grand piano. And here is that satellite photograph at a scale of 1:450, shot from a height of 705 kilometers, framed and hanging in the foyer, as though *National Geographic* had taken an interest in their lives.

Wesley watches the man and the dog playing below him. He watches impassively from a turn in the stair, studies them, thinking that soon he'll be expected to repeat certain motions, certain words and phrases. It's the memorization game at which he excels, and it begins like this.

The man says, "Speak!"

And the dog says, "Wuff!"

And the man says, "Good dog. Good boy! Come over here now. Come. Come. Sit. Good boy. Say your name."

And the dog says, "Wulf!"

"Oh God," Roger groans. "NO! NO! Come back here. Sit! Say your name. Say *Rex*."

And finally the dog says, "Rex."

"Good. Good dog. Now. Read this." He holds up a piece of paper.

The dog tilts his head, sniffs, listens. Wesley tilts his head, remembering, watching the woman who is watching both the man and the dog from a nearer distance.

"Read. This." Roger pronounces the words slowly and distinctly.

The dog blinks.

"READ!"

Without thinking, the dog says, "See Rex run."

"Okay, that's better," says the man. "Now read it again."

Rex makes an indefinite sound.

Then Roger hits him across the muzzle, a sharp downward blow that slaps the jaws together. "BAD! You're bad!" When he reaches to hit again, Rex cringes, tail between the legs and eyes tightly closed. "What is my name, for God's sake? Can you at least remember that?

Rex says, "What is my name."

"NO! NO! ROGER! Say *Roger*."

"Roger."

"Okay. Now read this."

"Can't," says Rex.

"Jesus Christ. This is ridiculous. He's hopeless, absolutely hopeless."

When Amy replies, she is soothing and rational. "Roger, please. Darling, you're the one who's hopeless. You just don't know how to work with him." She stoops, caresses the sharp and upright ears, runs her fingers through the gray-brown hair, the thick fur of his chest, giving a secret glance back toward the turning of the stair. "Good boy. Good Rex. All we want you to do is try. I know you can do it. Please try. Try hard for Amy. Good boy, goooooood boy. What does this say, fella? What does it say?"

The boy watches her. For a time only his fingers move, manipulating an imaginary controller, working an invisible joystick. She's acting, he thinks. She's acting for me.

Rex swallows and works his lips with effort. "Once upon a time."

The woman says, "Goooood! Good boy. You just have to be patient with him. That's all."

"He's an idiot," comes a disembodied male voice from the kitchen. "The whole thing is ridiculous."

"He's not an idiot. You just have to be patient. Rex, look at this. What does it say?"

"Once upon a time," says Rex, "there was a . . . a . . ."

"Wolf."

"Wolf."

"Gooood. Now keep going."

"A wolf. All skin and bone, so well did the. Dogs. Guard the, the. Neigh-bor-hood. Who met one moonshiney night a mas— mast—"

"Wesley," she says sweetly, without looking over her shoulder, "can you help Rex?"

"Mastiff," he says automatically.

"Good!" It is a short, sharp sound, almost an explosion of delight. She is so happy that her happiness fills the room.

Rex, though, had not noticed the boy, who had come partway down the stairs one moonshiney night. It had taken all of his concentration on the markings, and he had neither smelled nor heard Wesley on the stairs. Rex wagged and wiggled closer, radiating relief and happiness, licking the hand that held the book, and listening carefully now.

Amy continued, "Wesley, can you come down and help your friend? Can you come down and help Rex?"

"Sure." Wesley makes his way to the sofa and begins to read tonelessly. "The Wolf would gladly have supped off him but saw that first there would be a great fight, for which he was not prepared, and so he bid the dog good night very humbly. 'It would be very easy for you,' said the Mastiff, 'to get as fat as I am, if you liked. Quit this forest where you and your kind live so wretchedly and often die of hunger. Follow me, and you shall fare much better.'"

There is a tinkling of ice cubes from the kitchen and then Roger's tired voice. "This is ridiculous. It isn't helping either one of them. The whole story . . . it's far too elementary for Wesley, and—"

"Just be patient. I know what I'm doing."

"Yeah? Well, that dog gets one more chance, and that's it. You can handle it any way you want. But that's it." There is the sound of a door opening, and Roger's voice becomes fainter. "I'll be outside cleaning up. Somebody turned over the damn garbage cans again."

The door slams, and Amy pats both Wesley and Rex. "Wes, will you continue please."

Wesley thinks of the words as chords in a rather elementary composition. He plays them quickly, effortlessly. "'What shall I have to do,' said the Wolf. 'Almost nothing,' answered the Dog; 'only chase away the beggars and fawn upon the folks of the house.' The Wolf, at the thought of so much comfort, almost shed tears of joy. They trotted off together, but as they went along the Wolf noticed a bare mark on the Dog's neck. 'What is that mark?' said he. 'Oh nothing,' said the Dog."

It's all Amy can take of such drivel. She interrupts, thinking that perhaps she should have chosen a more modern story. "Thank you,

Wesley. Maybe we can let Rex finish. Rex, can you finish for us? Can you read, Rex?"

Rex hesitates, then continues. "'Nothing?' urged the Wolf. 'The merest tri—trifle,' answered the Dog. 'It is the mark of the collar where I am tied up at night.' 'Tied up!' ex . . . exclaimed the Wolf. 'You cannot run as you please?' 'Not always,' said the Mastiff, 'but what does it matter?' 'It matters to me,' re . . . rejoined the Wolf; and, leaping away, he ran once more to his native forest."

"Goooood! Good boy." Amy pats the head and leans back against the sofa, closing her eyes and massaging her temple. She sighs. "Now, Rex. Tell me, what does that story mean to you?"

"Story?"

"Yes. What does it mean to you?"

"I don't know."

"Try hard. It's important."

"Try, Rex," says Wesley. There is quick comprehension in his words, an understanding of consequences. "Try really hard. Please, Rex."

"I don't know."

"Oh. That's too bad. I'm sad now that you don't know what to think, Rex. I'm very sad." Her voice is sweet and caring.

"Rex, try really hard."

"I was hoping you would do better this time," she says. "But now . . . I'm sorry, Rex, I'm afraid you'll have to stay outside for awhile. I'm afraid you won't be able to spend the night in Wesley's room until you're able to do better."

"Mom, no."

"Here, Rex. Come along, boy."

"No, Mom, please."

There have been troubling developments since the death of their first son.

Sometimes there are whimpering sounds at night.

Urine stains on the carpet.

They have found unidentifiable tracks, dried mud, in several rooms of the house.

And savagely ripped articles of clothing left where someone will be sure to find them.

In the mornings Amy showers while Roger sleeps, then stands dripping in the doorway, shivering and staring at the recumbent form, the near stranger in her bed. Finally toweling herself, wrapping the towel around her body, and tucking one corner between her breasts, she steps before the mirror, standing where she can still see him and take in his every breath.

She begins brushing her hair with brisk, painful strokes that make her face flinch and set her jaw tightly shut.

But he is no longer asleep. And when he speaks, it sounds like the continuation of an old argument. His voice is tired. "Now what?"

"You're the one who wanted another child."

"I wanted a family. You wanted a child."

"Oh?" she replies flatly. "This is all my doing now?"

"I didn't say that." Their words have no more passion than the words of lawyers. "I'm just saying," Roger continues, "I'm just saying what do we do now? That's all I'm saying."

"I'm thirty-seven years old, Roger. Life has a way of closing in, you know?"

She dresses silently. In the hall mirror she ties the crème bow and then fluffs the ruffles on the front of her blouse. It is a pale silk blouse that contrasts sharply with the dark tan of her face. The effect is flattering, feminine, a look that will surprise both colleagues and students when she arrives on campus. They will stare and wonder if they have been misreading her after all.

Amy slips into the navy pumps and descends, throwing herself into the *Journal* with barely a good morning to Mrs. Dilettuso. By the time he joins her at the table, she has worked her way through the paper and moved on to a magazine. "I'll tell you what," she says. "Why don't you quit your job and stay home with him? Why don't you drive him to Little League and buy ice cream for the team?"

"Maybe I will," he says.

"Maybe you'd last a week. What do you want me to say, Roger? That this place needs a mommy? Maybe I should flush my career."

"No, I don't want you to say that. I don't know what I want you to say."

She avoids his glimpses.

They take their breakfast like communion. Bagels and jelly and juice.

Roger makes himself content with the early sun and the vista outside the breakfast room windows. The woods seem to draw him. It is a room full of white wicker furniture and uncertainty.

Toward the end Rex reaches them. Saves them perhaps. It begins with a clamor at the kitchen door, a frantic scratching to get out. And as soon as Roger opens the door, Rex bolts, eager to get at something lying just outside. There on the terrace is a legless corpse, covered with dirt and decay. It is a chunk of cloth barely recognizable as the rag doll it used to be. Rex takes hold with his teeth, the stuffing spilling out of his mouth like red and gray entrails, and Roger shivers, feels the food rising in his stomach. He barely has time to put out his foot and stop the crazy dog from dragging the thing into the kitchen.

Amy half turns from the refrigerator. "What is it? What's got him so excited?"

"It's Timmy," he says.

At first Wesley thinks of fairy tales, of goblins and ghosts, evil stepmothers and fathers who murder their sons, trolls burying small soft bodies in deep forest. And roots like crawling fingers that go down fast. It's like one of the stories from the book, but soon real patches of sunlight and the real warmth of afternoon banish dark thoughts. And Rex frolics. And they go walking, the three of them—Wesley, Roger, and Rex.

When the path fades, they follow a stream that trickles through their forest, turning with no regard for the straight and crooked of human perception. It is just a stream. After a time they go creekwalking. And when Rex at last plops belly down, head between his paws upon a sandbank, Roger and Wes practice construction. They make a dam of stones and sticks and creek clay. Then a waterfall. Then a bridge. And before long they cut sturdy branches for walking sticks and again go clambering over roots and rocks, working their way upstream for another hour or more into cooler, clearer water. Finally resting at a pool where water striders skate on the stretched-tight surface of late afternoon, finishing their snacks where the foliage is rubbery green and thick.

While they are walking and exploring, the stream begins to unravel imperceptibly, dividing itself, turning underground at one place and thinning to dribbles and drops in another. So they follow the dog, who scrambles thoughtlessly over moss boulders and through shadows, rips up a hillside of leaves, panting at the crest, the three of them panting and flopping together. And realizing by degrees that they are lost.

"This is great," says Roger. Then after a few breaths, "Reminds me of when I was a kid."

"You lived here?" The relief is audible in Wesley's voice.

"Naw. Just, you know, fooling around in the woods, doing guy stuff. I never knew all this was back here until old Rex"—he scratches Rex's ears—"showed us. It's great, isn't it?"

"How are we going to get back?" says Wesley.

Roger snaps a twig and throws both pieces. Rex pricks up his ears momentarily, sniffs, and begins rooting among the leaves. "Look at him. Not worried a bit, not losing a moment. That's the way we're going to be from now on. I promise."

"Does he know the way back?"

"This is great," Roger insists. "You can see the whole world from up here. Those houses look like mushrooms, don't they?"

"Is one of them our house?"

"I don't think so. Our house is probably over—that direction. Sort of that way. Don't worry, kiddo, all we got to do is find that creek again, right? Then follow the creek."

"I think it's going to be dark soon."

"You worry too much, son. Gotta learn to trust your instincts. Here, watch this. Yo, Rex! Rex! Come on, fella. Come here, boy. Rex! There, good boy. Take us on down to that creek, big fella. Take us on home."

Rex leads them downward through an arbor of winter jasmine as thick as vine-woven baskets. The sudden familiarity of the place, its quilt of curling leaves and its high canopy, conjure memories in Roger, leaving him momentarily confused, tilting and twirling with his thoughts. Looking up, he sees breaking buds of bright yellow that remind him of fireflies and summer evenings in the backyard of a house that was neither vast nor imposing. He smells hamburgers, hears his father and uncles laughing through crude stories, doing different voices and acting out the parts without even standing up. Remembers and returns to the present, where they hurry on, swishing through the leaves, following the dog in elaborate circles.

It is Wesley who notices the temperature dropping, the gathering darkness. Wesley who finds himself wishing for a trail of bread crumbs or a string to mark the way. Who notices Roger glancing furtively at his watch, and who thinks again of fairy tales.

They help each other over a fallen tree, then climb a small incline to get their bearings once more, and then, shrugging, follow Rex.

But it is Roger who realizes where they have arrived at last, who smells the jasmine and recognizes the dark-woven bower. And who understands that there will be no fireflies, no warm summer breeze. This time they drop down into the humus exhausted. And a familiar feeling, from all those years ago, washes over Roger's face and gathers in the corners of his eyes. He can't think of what to do, and perhaps for lack of a better thing he unbuttons the flannel shirt with shaking hands and wraps the boy in its warmth. "Jesus," he mutters to no one in particular, "what are we going to do now?"

"Dig," says Rex. "Dig."

In the dark of early morning Amy stands in a stinging spray that cannot wash away her fear. Even after she's wrapped herself in the silk robe, tied the knot with harsh jerks, she cannot stop shivering, like a diver anticipating not the cold plunge itself but the rocks just beneath the surface. So she goes walking, delicately, like a ghost, or like someone afraid of ghosts, to the round portal, where she brushes her hair and looks out upon a thousand shades of black. Afraid that any sudden movement might make her disappear.

A breezy ripple running through the grass reminds her of one summer spent in Scotland. Of Roger, ridiculous, staring out over Loch Ness at late evening, every day for a week, fully expecting something to emerge. And then, of course, losing faith. Thinking then and again now in the dim present, how like him. How like a man. So she brushes with the stiff strong brush, drawing it through her tangles with slow determination, almost welcoming pain. And in the entire house there is only the one light burning.

Until gradually she realizes what has happened.

Always a coward, just strong enough to steal, he's taken the boy and left.

Downstairs there'll be a note. The papers will come by Federal Express. Then he'll make an issue of everything in court, though he doesn't really want custody. He simply wants the power to bargain. He wants a clean break, a red sports convertible, a blonde girlfriend, an amicable divorce. Anything to make me hurt.

But by God I will keep this house, this one window where I can see with telescopic sight past the fraudulent lights below and the pathetic patterns of all their little lives. So that when she begins to cry, the tears are indistinguishable from droplets trickling off the handle of a brush held in her shaking hand. And at first she does not hear the sound at all.

There is a faint clicking of toenails across the tile floor below, a phantom movement in the kitchen, shuffling perhaps, which draws her down the stairs like someone already dead. Not even frightened anymore. Not even curious about what form the horror will take this time. Just drawn.

Almost sleepwalking now, with slow determination and only a vague sense of unreality, she turns the corner and flicks on the light, and they whirl from the vicinity of the refrigerator.

"We camped out!" Wesley screams.

They are pale and ragged, hollow eyed, covered with dirt and leaves. Newly dug from some grave.

She gasps, clutches the robe, and backs herself against the wall. They have filthy, hanging hair. Ragged nails and bloody fingers. Roger's eyes are a maze of broken capillaries, swollen flesh to the temples; his face is a chaos of stubble, scratches, and scrapes.

"I camped out!" he shouts again. "With Dad and Rex all night! We did it! We found the best place in the world and made a hole. And Rex kept us warm. All night!"

"Roger?"

"I don't know, I need . . . coffee, something."

"We told stories! We cuddled up with Rex under the leaves."

"Dear God. Are you hurt? Are you . . . are you okay? Look at you. Look at your clothes."

"I need something, I . . . a hot bath maybe. Some breakfast."

Amy drops the brush, begins to undress them, stops to wipe a cut, to pick leaves from Wesley's hair. Scolds and cries, the back of one hand pressed to her lips. Jerks their filthy clothing away and makes a pile before shooing them upstairs to steaming hot water and antiseptic. She hunts out clean towels and underwear. Pours forth a breathless litany of questions and recriminations. What in God's name was he trying to prove? Alone with a child, no camping equipment, no precautions of any sort. When you could have frozen to death. Letting that dog back in the house like this. Ticks and lice. People have died for God's sake. There has to be a rational explanation. Roger. Roger, what in God's name were you thinking? What was going on inside your mind?

"Nothing," he says. "I just . . . I don't know."

She hovers, waiting for an explanation that never comes.

Overturns a flower arrangement on one of her trips down the stairs, looking for clean socks perhaps or fabric softener or something, which falls from her mind as soon as she sees the new thing. It stops her, leaves her breathless one last time, like the magician's grand finale. And she, like the beautiful assistant, takes it up in her hand and holds forth the wonder. Across the seat of her chair in the kitchen, someone has left her a sprig of winter jasmine, as thin and ragged as honeysuckle, as yellow and bright as a star.

Food Is Fuel

1

In the tale of the Japanese magician, the year is 1939, and the nightclub is a renovated mansion called The Oasis. It's owned by Robert Hassard. The opening scene has Robert gliding from table to table, greeting his guests like an election-year politician, and it's a comforting moment. The men are in tuxedos. The women, after they have been undraped, are in a profusion of sequins and ostrich feathers. They glimmer and shine in spite of the freezing rain outside, and soon everyone has been warmed by the orchestra's own rendition of Tommy Dorsey's "Little White Lies." There's polished brass everywhere you turn. Leaded crystal and white gloves. In fact, the only detail that seems out of place in this part of the story is the one involving the cocktail waitresses. The girls of The Oasis wear tight satin shorts and white satin blouses, and they go wiggling between the tables with a sensuality not ordinarily associated with the thirties. Still, it's the year of *Gone with the Wind*. Two years since the Hindenburg disaster. And anything seems possible. There are even rumors that Tommy and Jimmy Dorsey are getting back together.

2

The orchestra swings into "Beale Street Blues" just as Robert passes a darkened table in one of the alcoves. It is of course my table, and he notices me because I am the author and my sudden appearance has given him a start. So naturally Robert hesitates, but at last he extends a soft, unformed hand. "Jack," he manages to say, "how are you?"

"Fine, Robert. How's business?"

"Great. Really great. What are you doing here?" Though he knows very well what is happening.

He knows because the young woman with me is roughly half my age—much thinner than she would be in an ordinary story—with a wide, sensuous mouth and dark hair done in a style that Robert has never seen before. She looks altogether too fragile to bear the weight she will be asked to bear over the next few pages, like one of those Polish refugees we keep seeing in the newsreels. Her dark eyes have a distance about them that frightens Robert since he knows I've brought her here for sex, as I've done in earlier stories, though he himself cannot imagine making love to anything so frail.

"I want you to meet Claire," I say.

So Robert frowns as usual, takes another step into the darkness, and extends his hand once again. "How do you do, miss. Welcome to The Oasis."

After they touch and he's left staring at his palm, I say, "Relax, Robert. Why don't you tell us what you have on stage tonight."

"Oh, yeah . . . yeah. I think you're going to like this, Jack. It's a magician. Japanese guy, you know. He does stuff with food. Really outrageous stuff, like he cooks children or something." Robert laughs twice and looks to see if anyone is noticing our conversation.

"Really?" I take a slow drink and savor the sting before swallowing. Then look out over the crowd for the one face that could change all this. And find nothing. "I don't know, Robert. I may need to make some changes."

Then I look at the girl and pat her hand.

3

In reality I am back in the hospital room after a long day of tests, some-where between "liquids only" and a dawn that doesn't seem to be im-minent. I look across at my daughter, who is about half my age, and the thought that she might have some connection to Claire, however tenuous, makes me nauseated. So I try to redirect my thoughts. The whole thing is unsteady in my mind, and finally I say, "Ann Marie—I have something to give you. I've been thinking about it for a long time."

She straightens in the chair, blinks herself back into the room, and finds a voice that's husky and slow after hours of almost sleep. She's pretty and plump, my daughter, like all of those actresses before the war, and I see her the way I see Judy Garland—perfect—in the Land of Oz. She is a sweet girl, innocent of any imagination that could threaten her. "You'll be home in a couple of days, Pop. You can give it to me then."

"Maybe not. You never used to call me Pop."

"What does that mean?"

"It means you must think I'm going to die."

"Well, . . . Jack, . . . that's ridiculous." She stretches and yawns, then makes a pocket for her feet in the blanket and nestles again into one corner of the chair. "You just have a big day tomorrow, and you should get some sleep. I think we should both get some sleep. It's two AM."

I push the buttons, and something under the bed whirs, bending me into the shape of a W. "I like this," I say. "I feel like an astronaut, you know, re-entering the atmosphere or something."

"It's two AM, Pop. They're scheduled to operate at six."

"This won't take long. Just give me a sip of water. I want to tell you a story. Story about a Japanese magician."

Without looking at the window, that useless mirror, I already know what is happening outside in the hospital parking lot. I can just tell. I'm that good at imagining this sort of thing. So I'm certain that there are two security guards, cupping their coffee in both hands, a young woman, and an older man on the sidewalk next to the emergency ramp. And for a reason that I can't yet articulate, they remind me of characters out of Hemingway—maybe I'll hit upon it later, the proper allusion—but at the moment, in the resinous present, I know for sure that these two guards go their way tottering like penguins. And I know that there are broad sheets of runoff on the concrete, freezing rain that's layering itself into transparencies that reflect streetlights into crooked shapes. It's a monstrous night. And I know that the only other person in the parking lot is a bundled nurse, impatient to get home after her shift, who cannot wait for her car's defroster to work. And that she reaches one hand to the windshield and scrubs wild circles until—just for an instant—she can see perfectly into my second-floor room. And she thinks, good God, are we ever going to see flowers like that again? And then puts her car into gear. While inside the room itself, I'm mentioning to my daughter that the story of the Japanese magician takes place on a night very much like this one. And she sighs. Just like her mother, for whom she is named.

4

When midnight arrives, the Japanese magician does indeed take the stage and goes through the usual flourishes, except with a difference, a little twist on the conventions. It's what makes him special. Take the dove trick, for instance, something we think we've seen a thousand times. It works like this in the hands of Hadashi, the Japanese magician:

As he draws off his white glove, one finger at a time, he gives it a snap and produces, not the fluttering dove we expect, but a luna moth, which perches on the tip of one finger. He pretends to stroke the creature with his free hand and walks it through the loops and swirls of some imaginary flight while the moth sits serenely, tilting its wings from time to time to keep its balance. Then Hadashi faces us, bows, and brings his hands together in a single explosive clap. The moth disappears, and in its place there is a paper fan which, when opened, reveals the pale green image of a luna moth. Then, with a flick, the fan is gone, and the real moth reappears, its long swallowtails and delicate kimono wings unwrinkled by the transformation. This time Hadashi tosses it into the air, letting it make a single stuttering circle before alighting again on his finger like a trained animal. I applaud, not because of the magic, but because of the choreography. Hadashi is as graceful as a dancer.

Claire applauds.

Gradually the spotlight narrows, and the magician lifts from his black table a long samurai sword, unsheathed with a hiss and inserted into the light with one upswung stroke. Then Hadashi raises the moth to his lips for a farewell kiss before setting it to flight. It makes the same uncertain circle as before and seems at first to alight on the gleaming point of the *katana*. The wings, though, never stop fluttering. I assume it's merely a problem of balance until gradually I come to understand. The creature is impaling itself.

For a long time it struggles, its task made more difficult by the increasing width of the blade. For a moment I slip back into the story itself, amazed at how diligent the moth is, how like a bird it beats its wings against the resisting steel. And how like a fairy tale it dies. Hadashi's hand never falters though. Claire and I are seated close enough to the scene—or perhaps this is only my imagination—that we can see the glistening point as it breaks through the animal's back. Still, it takes an eternity for the wings to stop beating, a time during which the spotlight shrinks into an even narrower column of light, until at last we see only the pale hand of the master, the cold silver blade, and the slowly stiffening wings.

When the spotlight widens, Hadashi is with us again, smiling his slight smile and passing the sword to an assistant. Then he places a hibachi on his table and makes a fire with another snap of his fingers. Burns a strip of rice paper to show the fire is real. Next he takes off his coat and replaces it with a chef's apron before setting an ordinary skillet into the flames. All of this he does without a word, letting the fire do its work until he has a dab of butter sizzling in the pan, adding, after a moment, a handful of sugar and a touch of sherry as the mixture begins to caramelize. Then lets the blaze lick higher, tilting the skillet this way and that until crackling blue flames halo the edges. And then, with one smooth motion, he swallows the moth between lid and pan. Just like that.

It is at this point that I become more fully conscious of Claire. What I mean is that I realize I've left her without a significant role in the story so far, not even a reaction to the magician's act. So I listen for her words as Hadashi snatches the lid away and flips the contents into the air, the moth flying once again beautifully, radiantly into the upper darkness, while I seem to hear her saying something about home, going home. And I begin to think that my idea of amusement might be a bit droll for someone just out of her teens.

"There's no need to be upset," I assure her. "It's just an illusion. Just a moth. And anyway"—I try to make her smile—"they do it to the women all the time."

"Do what, Jack?"

"The magicians. They stick 'em with swords."

"I think I want to go home."

That makes me pause. Finally I ask, "When you say you want to go home, do you mean to my place? Or home to your parents . . . in New Orleans?"

5

Now I can tell she's all out of patience, and why not? Yesterday she flew a thousand miles to spend the night in a pink cheap motel near the hospital in order to be with me today because I have no wife, no other children, and the weight falls where it always does. I can see the tightening of her shoulders and the clenching of the jaw and the deep,

deep breath she takes. "Pop," she exhales at last. "Do you want me to see if they'll give you something to make you sleep?"

"Why would you do that?"

"It's okay to be nervous. You just need to save your strength."

"I'm not nervous."

"They do this operation all the time. It's almost routine."

"What are you talking about?"

"Your story. It was just a dream, or maybe the medication. Anyhow—I think your imagination was giving you a picture of yourself as Claire. Who naturally wants to go home, because you're somewhere you've never been before and it's a little unfamiliar and a little frightening. But it's going to be okay. I promise."

"This is what they taught you in graduate school?"

"Pop, there wasn't a Japanese magician. Dr. Hadashi is your doctor. I met him yesterday. In this room. Here."

"You're telling me how to write my own story?"

"Your 'magician' was using a scalpel, and even in your dream the moth 'came back to life,' didn't it? It's going to be okay."

So this is to be our Thanksgiving and Christmas, is it? The long sleepy interlude after the feast when we plop down in stuffed comfort and talk. Like families. Only now she's telling me I'm a coward. And I am in one sense. But this isn't going to be the dream story she suspects, not by any measure. It's something else entirely. And what I'm trying to confess is that after the marriage to her mother failed and the novel succeeded—shortly after that combined tragedy—I began taking my students to lunch. That's what I'm trying to tell her.

Only now I'm wondering if she realizes that Hadashi is the same surgeon who operated on her mother. And that that's why I chose him. We live in such a small space, after all, and for such a short time. We have to expect these coincidences. I wonder if that's occurred to her yet.

6

I first met Claire from the bed of one of her housemates. What I mean of course is that they all shared a bungalow on Charles Street and treated me, the four of them, with a nonchalance that seemed at the time like a holdover from the sixties. I was Jack. They were sweet. And what was the harm of it until the one crisp November morning when I raised myself on one elbow, still in the musky warmth of Katie and the previous night, to uncover enough of a coincidence to make the story of the Japanese magician into tragedy: Claire and I both had early classes. She was the dark one. The tall thin one who looked like a movie director's idea of an art major — large, liquid eyes and a face too intelligent for her to be cast simply as "housemate number two."

Then, after I rubbed my face and untangled some of the bedcover, I found her still in the hallway, still staring at me and made beautiful by a morning light too delicate to cast a shadow. And so I suggested, "Hi?"

"Hi," she said. Like someone encountering a foreign language.

Why was I surprised? It was her house after all, and I was the stranger struggling to get his feet on the floor and taking care to rearrange the sheets over the bare shoulders lying next to me and sniffing and rubbing my face again like an old drunk. And she had every right to stare the way they stare when they think they're safe. When they reach that dangerous plateau where you can actually see them thinking "we're all adults here."

"You need to use the bathroom first?" she asked.

"Ah, no. You go ahead."

There. As simple as that. My moment of unfaithfulness to Katie, with whom I had been unfaithful to Ashley, with whom I'd been unfaithful to Ann Marie, my wife. It would be the moment in the film of my life in which the camera crept close and tried to find some flicker · of a decision working its way across my face. Except that there isn't any decision of course, just a need to find something I had been searching for. Trying to clear my head and maybe even to determine if her robe really was hanging open and if it was the thinness of her thighs or my own imagination that vastly exaggerated her sex. This was the moment when I dropped my eyes and spoke so softly that I *must* have known it was already a secret between us. Like a man enslaved.

Later, downstairs, we shared bagels and juice. She had transformed herself. In the fairy tale it would have been into a princess, I suppose. Here, a fashion model. While I had stuffed myself into jeans and T-shirt, the motley of middle age. We talked in conspiratorial voices, stumbling past the awkwardness of it all until she said something like "you're the writer, right?" and maybe giggled. I'm not sure.

"Yeah," I said, because a *yes* would have been unbelievable, "a literary genius." And then I did the eyebrow thing and crooked a smile, saying, "Do you see my socks over there somewhere, maybe on the floor?" Which is what convinced her, I believe. Not flowers or fancy words. Socks. Because women really don't believe in the ritual of romance. They believe in breakfast. That's the secret, I have found. Letting them see that you're watching them eat, caressing their food with your eyes. Marriages have been made on less.

Except then I heard myself saying, "Katie and I are having lunch at the Depot. You want to come along?"

And her saying, "Why?" Not one of the responses I had anticipated.

"I'm working on a story. And I was wondering if you'd be interested. Either of you. Or both."

Claire drew back an inch and smiled polite incomprehension. How could she know what I meant? I hardly knew myself.

"It's a story about food," I improvised.

She stopped chewing. Swallowed and hardened her eyes, showing, I suppose, that you can carry this silliness too far.

"Not about food actually, but a chef. I'm basing it on a real person. Named Hadashi. Who has a reputation for giving performances that are a bit over the line. Dinner extravaganzas, that sort of thing. He cooks children or something."

Claire spread butter on her bagel, bit, and chewed provocatively. "Hmmm. What does he really do?"

"A little magic, a little culinary art, a little pornography. At times I think he can be a bit indelicate, so if you're put off by . . ."

"He's some kind of performance artist, right?"

"Look, the only thing I know for certain is that there's sex above and below and inside of everything we put into our mouths. . . ." I waited, and she waited with me to see how this new silliness would end. "And that your other housemate, Samantha . . ." I drew my finger through the faint film of grease coating the tabletop, making an elegant snail's path that stopped in front of her plate, where I pressed down hard, then lifted, so that the residual stickiness tugged at the skin of my fingertip. ". . . and her friend Jamie were making love on this table exactly one minute before you sat down."

She laughed out loud.

Perhaps that was when I fell in love. I don't know. It was hard to tell at the time, and I was as vacant as an empty room. I knew that Claire was one of the little literary girls who hang around every literary event at every college in the country. Then disappear. So I must have known from the start that I would lose her. I just didn't know what it would mean. I suppose I thought the story itself would save me.

I mean, if you're the writer . . . right?

7

Hadashi did not look beyond our table when he asked for volunteers. And he was reaching out his hand even before Claire rose up from her seat. Whispering to her while she ascended the stairs, as if I had nothing at all to do with this part of the story. My friend Robert, always on the periphery of darkness, stood close enough that I could see the confusion, then the alarm, spreading across his face.

"I thought she wanted to go home," I shrugged.

He gave me a tense smile, Robert did, and then slipped away to the bar, where he engaged one of the waitresses in conversation, both of them glancing at me from time to time. Though I gave them nothing in return. My eye stayed upon Hadashi and the magic he was working in the delicate light that I had seen somewhere before.

When he hypnotized her, it was like a courtship. He did it without orb or pendulum, just soft words and slight touches of the hand, caressing her shoulder as he whispered, lifting one of the wavelets of her hair—all the things that I myself had not thought to do. And soon she was asleep, responding occasionally with a murmur or a moan too private to be translated. Until finally Hadashi lifted Claire's hand into the light, where it seemed to float. Then he lowered it, soothing her body at the same time with those wavering motions of his hand. Then he brought his face closer to hers and gave her the same kiss he had given the moth.

I had to blink to convince myself I had not been hypnotized as well.

During this interlude a mute, faceless corps of attendants began to rearrange the stage. They transformed the empty space into an imaginary banquet hall, with pasteboard columns and crumbling arches. The veils and tapestries of a castle. A wooden table as long as a ship—one chair at either end and a vast expanse between. All of this accomplished against a backdrop of half a dozen figures straining to roll a crude new shape onto center stage, a machine of some sort, an iron engine with levers and dials and hinged doors leaking an orange glow. It was as massive as a locomotive and, very soon, as loud. What it gave out was the rush of a blowtorch, and what we saw inside, through the one low portal, was a hurricane of fire.

Then four more attendants emerged, carrying on their shoulders a metal tray, which they lowered onto the banquet table. It looked like a shallow coffin, blackened by fire and dented by long use, its meaning made more obscure by the last figure to leave the stage, who emptied two buckets of water into its length. The whole scene was like watching a circus, our eyes flitting among dark impressions and being drawn back inevitably to the one figure whose slightest movement suggested new illusions and new meanings. And it was not long before he had refocused our attention by making the most mundane of gestures. Hadashi took up a pair of scissors from his table of props and raised them above his head, making several snips into the air. Nothing mysterious, he seemed to be saying. Scissors. Just like the ones you use at home.

Then he stepped behind Claire, making with his left hand a sweeping gesture as if to offer, ladies and gentlemen, an appreciative view.

Then raised the scissors again with his right hand and gave two distinct snips above her head. The blades sliced through the air, and Claire's dress fell to her feet. Then her underclothing, rings, watch, and necklace fell away with the second snip. I saw it and did not doubt the magic, because I already knew the truth of her. Her breasts hardly noticeable except for their delicate whiteness. Her body straight and sad. A pillow of thick, dark hair where her legs met. She was as frail and lovely as a luna moth. And as cold and quiet as a corpse.

Hadashi stiffened the fingers of one hand and by degrees levitated her, suspending Claire, the girl who wanted to go home, above the metal coffin. Then lowered her with barely a ripple. The rest was either frightening or not, because of its familiarity. He used the same sword that he had used before. And he moved in a sort of ballet. Slicing the fruit and floating it next to her body. Scattering chrysanthemum petals over her breasts. Adding plums, peaches, water chestnut, and mushrooms. Coating her with honey and caressing the unresisting form of her. Then kissing the apple and planting it deeply between her legs. Until at last he gave a final, soothing pass of the hand as if to urge her into a deeper sleep. And the metal lid descended, and was clamped shut. The assistants carried her the way they would have carried a casket, opened the iron lips of the oven, and let the flames lick forth. It was Hadashi himself who shoved her into the inferno.

And then we waited.

There were more tricks of course, more spectacles. Perhaps an hour of them, I'm not sure. My eyes found their occupation among the orange and blue flames. Until finally. They drew her forth again and set the sarcophagus upon the banquet table once more. Someone poured water over the lid, creating an immense cloud of steam that drifted over us, the audience. A man with quilted gloves unclamped the lid, and Hadashi himself lifted the cover, his face obscured by more escaping steam. Then he dipped a ladle into the mixture, tasted it ruefully, smiled. And we smiled with him. We were amused. It was all so absurd.

He had transformed her into an old woman, a sleeping spinster with boiling liquid gurgling all about her. The skin had cracked and peeled in places, turned shiny and dark in others. Her belly had grown soft and swollen, while vague strips of flesh hung loosely at her hips and thighs. It was marvelous, said a woman at a near table, as real as a roasted turkey: no one is more exacting than the Japanese magician. There was ripe applause as people stood on tiptoe to get their look—skin pulling away from wrist and ankles, the hair on her head and the now tiny patch between her legs looking as though it had been spun from sugar, charred, and some of it burned away. It was all too much, they agreed. Not a detail left undone. Even the face had its perfect sheen, the surface drawn back by the fire's delicate fingers and melded to the skull. The lips as though they had been sewn shut. The eyes like varnished slits. And nervous laughter all around.

It took a moment for Hadashi to silence the crowd, but, as Robert had said, we had given ourselves over to the perfect showman, and he was insistent upon his final effect.

He reached out his hand and clutched the air, pulling invisible strings toward him; and the body began to stir. The woman in the coffin raised one knee slightly and moaned, some of the liquid sloshing, sizzling against the sides. The head turned to face us, and one of the eyes cracked open. She seemed to be examining her own arm like a mummy just awakening from its long sleep, but I do not think she was surprised by the crumbling flesh. I think she was looking at me, searching for something I could not give or say. And it was the Japanese magician who kissed her hand and laid it gently over her breast and brushed her lips with his own.

When the lights came on again, the stage was clear.

8

What I have discovered is that the floor of my hospital room is as bright and chitinous as a beetle's shell. When I look down, I see my face floating several inches beneath a surface of stone, distorted, like moonlight stretched across water. Maybe that's the way she sees me now. Or maybe that's the way she sees my story, because she's looking down herself, and the blanket has slipped from her lap and made itself into a mountainous island upon a faraway sea. And the face that she has found, I suspect, is not mine, but her mother's face. I think she's beginning to understand.

"Why would you make up something like that?" she said. "Why would you tell me a story like that?"

"Because I never fell out of love with her. Ever."

"You divorced her. And then she died."

"Of breast cancer, two years, three months, and six days after. I know. That's why I'm telling you what really happened."

"It's not going to happen to you."

"No, I'm not afraid of that. What I'm trying to tell you is that, shortly before your mother died . . ."

"Look, you don't have to do this."

". . . I began taking my students to lunch."

"Pop . . ."

"I would put them into my stories—it would never amount to much—and they would be sweet and delicious for a while. Then they would drift away. Marry their young men. It certainly wasn't real to me, and I doubt that it was for them. But each time they drifted away, there was this little pinprick that reminded me of something."

"Is that what happened with Claire?"

"I suppose."

"And it reminded you of what?"

"That I was famous for a while. After that first book. Then the novel came along, and I developed a taste for the real thing. It's what fame will do; I'm just surprised at how little it took. To ruin things, I mean."

"You don't need to do this, Jack."

"You've got a family, a real family. You can do better."

"You don't have to do any of this."

"I know. I'm just trying to tell you where I've been for the past ten years. Besides, how was I supposed to know it was a love story?"

"Go back to sleep. I'll be there when you wake up."

"The trick, you see, is to face all this without falling into sentimentality. That's the trick. I just . . . I loved her so much."

9

"You mind if I ask you something, Jack?"

I can hear Robert's voice, and when I open my eyes, I can see his lugubrious face. He reminds me of Bogart just after the plane leaves. Every time I come to the club I expect to see him in a gray fedora and double-breasted suit, except that would be too informal. Robert is a tuxedo man. The starched shirt, the satin stripe and satin lapels seem to hold him together, to frame his overriding decency in a way that words cannot. And for the first time, in any version of the story, I wonder what I look like to him. Maybe like a drunk just lifting his head from the bar.

"What . . . ?"

"You okay?"

"Yeah, I'm okay. Where is everybody?"

"Gone."

"The kid I was with?"

"You took her home, Jack. You don't remember that?"

"No. How about Hadashi?"

"Gone. They're all gone. I mean, hell, Jack, it's your story. You're telling me you don't know what happens?"

"Is that what you were going to ask?"

"No. No, as a matter of fact, I was going to ask why you picked the thirties. I mean, you weren't even alive then, right?"

"I don't know. I suppose I thought it was safe—innocent or something. The time before the war and all that. Maybe stories I heard from my parents. I don't know."

"Because, you know, what it looks like from this side . . . kind of like it's all starting to unravel on you."

"Just tell me one thing, Robert. Do you remember a cocktail waitress named Ann Marie?"

"That's who you're looking for, somebody named Ann Marie?"

"Yeah."

Robert walks behind the bar and selects a half-empty bottle from among the rows. Balances two glasses in the palm of his hand. "Nope. I don't remember anybody by that name. And I remember 'em all; it's my job."

"That's too bad."

One of the waiters has upended the last of the chairs, and now the tables all look as if they're wearing crowns. Someone is sweeping near the piano. And someone else is wringing out a mop, then making long liquid strokes, turning the floor into a reflecting pool. There's a hint of daylight around the window frames, maybe enough to suggest that the night is finally over. Robert pours two drinks and slides one in my direction.

"Tell me something else, Jack. Back there when you said you were going to make some changes . . ." He raised his glass in my direction, then took a sip with his eyes closed. Popped his lips apart and planted his elbows on the bar. "What was that all about?"

I raised my own glass, and we took another long drink together. Finally he understood.

"I'll be taking over the club myself for a while."

"Ah."

"I appreciate everything you've done, Robert. I really do."

"Yeah. Thanks."

"It's getting a little late, I realize that. And I'm sorry, I really am."

"It's okay, Jack. You don't have to be sorry."

"It's just something I have to do."

"Yeah." He finished his drink and came out from behind the bar. We shook hands in front of the stage where Hadashi had worked his magic.

I was afraid at first that Robert would not see the door, but I need not have worried. Like all great politicians, my good friend had known from the first how to take his exit. He straightened his jacket and, from a distance of eight or ten feet, gave a modest wave as he turned toward the corridor. Walking a bit stiffly perhaps. But, unless I am very much mistaken, Robert Hassard gave me a quick wink as he faced the long hall; then, smoothing back his hair just as Bogart would have done, he fronted the door and reached for its handle. There was a cold light that fanned out across the floor and a vague movement on the other side of the threshold. Then he was gone.

The sweeper went back to his sweeping. I rocked the ice in my glass and thought that, if he had only asked, I would have gladly walked with him into the light.

Abduction

Here's a flash. If I phone them, it's a story. If they phone me, it's therapy. No exceptions. And that's the tabloid truth. So usually I say this—I ask 'em, I say, you got pictures? You got some way I can verify this crap? And then of course about half of them hang up. The other half are inventive. It's why I throw away my life in Best Western parking lots, isn't it? Waiting for Elvis or some woman with a two-headed baby. Because you never know.

So, anyhow, this kid's cracking the door just enough to show one of those flannel granny gowns. Pink damn flowers from neck to ankle, one hand on the knob and one on the chain like some old lady who's suddenly got second thoughts about turning in the Satan worshiper across the street. And I'm outside in what passes for a hallway thinking, okay, okay, at least you believe, while I flash her some ID and start crooning. "Hi. I'm Barry Nussbaum. From the *Global-Star?*"

And nothing. I mean nothing.

She's got herself wedged behind the door, trying to decide whether to slam or trust some old guy with a ponytail and loose tie. Like maybe I've come to take her back to the mother ship. Who the hell knows what she's seeing? So I back off, smile, try to see what it is that *I'm* seeing; and it's not a story. She looks about fifteen. Big honey blonde hair that hasn't seen a brush in two days, blue eyes that are way past bloodshot, and not quite enough makeup to ruin a perfect complexion. Probably a runaway. And I'm thinking, Jesus, she looks like a cheerleader that somebody beat the shit out of. Except that's not news and I'm already into my routine. "Janelle? Are you the Janelle Roberts who called? Because, honey, if you've got a story, I can't get it out here in the corridor. Now, do you want to talk to the cops or do you want to talk to me?" Pure bluff, but it gets the door open, doesn't it?

"I can't stop crying," she says.

Okay. I'm inside now, and it's real. The stale air. Food cartons on the floor, trash talk on the tube. And I feel this tightness in my chest, this familiar, sad fatigue that's going to drag me into some trailer park and kill me someday. I can tell she's freaked out. Got the furniture arranged around her bed like a barricade, Pooh Bear against the head-board, rose petals all over the nightstand like the flower girl went crazy at your cousin's wedding. Draperies closed. And I can feel the flu coming on, everything going numb including my emotions, and I have to concentrate just to taste the cigarette smoke — exhale, watch it drift. And here we are. She's looking at me; I'm looking at her pink toenails. Like we're the most normal couple in the world.

"You mentioned a boyfriend over the phone?"

I'm just treading water. I saw there was nothing for the front page in the first ten seconds, and I've already reduced her to a six-inch piece in the back — if I can find the angle. We avoid each other's faces and stare instead into this pile of crumpled sheets in the corner. It's the way they all do. Like they're trying to tell you something by telepathy.

Finally she says, "He's gone. I think he took the car." Easing her feet under this green blanket that looks like pond scum, then drawing her knees up the way they do when they're little girls.

So I just come right out with it, my one foray into cleverness. "Look, is he the one who hit you?"

But she shakes her head, puzzled. So I fish out the tape recorder and figure I'll give her ten more minutes because, underneath, she's beautiful, and I feel like she's somebody I knew and lost a long time ago. So I ask her if she's called anyone else.

"No," she says. "I just need the money."

And I think, God, you could be an actress. You could be Lolita. You could be my own kid, somebody I loved if the world weren't such a garbage heap, but instead I hear myself saying, "Okay. Here's the deal. You get a thousand dollars straight up if I can verify what you say. Five thousand if I get photographs. But you've got to convince me. We don't pay for scams, and we don't do counseling. So, Janelle. Have we got an abduction story or not?"

"Last night," she nodded.

"Good. Good. Now—amaze me."

"There was this rumbling noise, like a train. And then this bright light. You know, like . . . a train."

"Okay, forget the recorder. Just talk to me."

"I couldn't move. It was like I was floating, up, but I couldn't move, and then I was just there."

"Where? In a room? A spacecraft?"

"I don't know."

"Okay, don't worry about that. We can do a sketch later. Now, after you were lifted up, is that when you saw the alien?"

"Yes, I mean, no. I didn't have any clothes on, and I couldn't move. I don't remember exactly. It was so cold, and they made me lay back."

"That's when they examined you?"

"Yes."

Now I want to pick her up and shake her, shake the damn flowers off her gown and say, You think I haven't heard this before? You think I'm paying for this? Sweetie, I've written this same story a hundred and forty-six different ways. I know who tells it, and I know who reads it. And I can get your whole life into three paragraphs.

But I hear her whispering to me, "Mr. Nussbaum, I'm afraid I'm going insane."

"Let's open the drapes; it's still light outside."

"No!"

"Okay, but tell me what really happened."

Tears now. She's winding the bedspread around her legs and shivering. Backing away now.

"Janelle, listen to me. I can smell a phony before it gets cooking. It's part of my job. Now if you need some kind of help—"

"There was an alien."

"Look, I've got to go. Is there somebody you want me to call?"

"There was! A person."

"Okay. There was an alien. What did he look like?"

"He was so small."

"Okay, small. What else?"

"A large head, very large. And those eyes just like the pictures. Round but, you know, pointed at the end. These deep dark eyes. And tiny little hands, Mr. Nussbaum. I'm not imagining this."

"What else?"

"Just this little gash, this purple gash for a mouth. And no hair. No hair on its body. Please. Please, help me."

I flick off the recorder. "Look, whoever you are, I'm really sorry. I know you're confused and that somebody's hurt you—okay? I'll call Social Services when I get back to the office. Here's a twenty; it's all I've got."

"It was gray!" Defiance? I can't tell, and it doesn't make any difference—what does anybody named Janelle Roberts have to defy? "Sort of pinkish gray. A little bit . . . bluish gray, I think. I couldn't . . . watch."

"Just one?"

"Yes."

"Well, maybe you were dreaming." It's the kindest thing I can think to say.

"You weren't there."

"I know. Good-bye."

"You weren't there when it cried."

"What?"

"When it made this crying sound. When it came out."

"When it came out of . . . ?"

"After it came out of me."

It takes a moment for me to realize.

"It made this tiny sound. And the eyes made real tears, so I knew it was from somewhere, but I just couldn't. I couldn't go back, and it couldn't go back, but it was real. It was from somewhere. So I took the pillow. To make it stop."

"Jesus Christ."

"And wrapped it in the sheets. Over there in the corner. You know, for the pictures."

And when I finally reach out, she settles into my arms.

The Guardian

FOR MILES

Okay, we're flying low now, delivering this bigmother Easter arrangement in the old panel truck looks like a hearse, decal across the back
saying WEISS FLORIST — FTD 205 South Main Street in Morton WE
DELIVER inside a black ivy wreath, which maybe should have been a
red cross, on account of that's the way we work. Elrod's up front fighting to keep us between the lines. I'm in the back holding this purple
and white bastard looks like an Indian headdress, ducking when we
round corners so I don't get whanged by one of the swinging metal
hooks we load casket sprays on. Thing must weigh thirty-five, forty
pounds except for the short periods of zero gravity when we go air-
borne, and it's a little top heavy too on account of the Easter lilies, but
do they ever think about that back at the shop? Hell no.

So it's inevitable. I mean we're headed south on Hwy. 115, right?
Toward Baxter. Low cloud ceiling, visibility less than ten miles, and
me without a parachute. Comes to the railroad crossing in front of the
big denim plant, and what does the son of a bitch do? Takes the ramp
like he was Fireball Roberts and this was his last chance at the leap of
death. Then, voom, right out on the floor. The water, the Styrofoam,
the peacock feathers, the ferns, and every kind of purple and white
flower in the jungle, all over the inside of that green ratty-assed panel
truck, and me screaming, "Holy shit! They fell out, El, they're floatin'

out the back of the truck," but he keeps going like he's got plenty of fuel and just enough time for one more bomb run.

So what do you do? I mean, you're fourteen years old. The guy is retarded. You got an altar arrangement looks like it's been thrown up against a wall, and this is your first real life honest to God paycheck-paying job, which you deserve only because your mamma works there in the first place. And maybe his sister does own the flower joint and maybe you really are just a kid, but that won't change a thing because you're responsible for whatever happens next. Age doesn't have anything to do with it. So you've got to communicate in terms he can comprehend, right? "El! Hit the brakes, man! Oh God, we gotta go back. Jeezus Christ, El, it looks like somebody vomited flowers back here. I think I peed my pants."

"Pull over?"

"You not hear what I'm saying? The sum bitch exploded. We look like a free love bus turned wrong side out."

"Can't," he moans. At least that's what I think he says. The wind's catching everything and whirling it around me like a tornado.

"Oh God! El, you gotta listen to me, man. This ain't a cavalry charge; we in the florist bidness!"

"Church ladies gone meet us five o'clock. Then we got the hospital run."

It was the way he thought. Sort of like he'd got tuned in real good and clear on this one channel and didn't care to switch. Not retarded exactly, I take that back, but pretty damn focused on the here and now, if you know what I mean. Somebody told me he learned how to drive in the air force during the Korean War, though he didn't climb high in the ranks. They gave him a job trucking aviation fuel where the casualty rate was higher than actual combat.

And now here we are pulling up to the curb at Baxter Presbyterian, dripping and smoking right in the shadow of the steeple. El eases out from behind the wheel like he's the only Elrod Weiss in kingdom come and it didn't pay to hurry it any. And me, I'm trying to breathe. I'm pulling myself out of the water by one of the hooks, and I can see them through the side window, flouncing down the walk, the kind of foul-tempered biddies who show up Saturday afternoon dressed for church and wanting to inspect the big altar arrangement because they're on the Worship Committee or some damn thing and 100 percent ready to peck you to death, boy, if one leaf is out of place. That kind. Holding their pocketbooks out front like this. Lips that haven't touched nothing but lemon juice in the past twenty years. And me in the back believing in the power of prayer with all my heart.

So. He gets the door about half open and starts picking up flowers, no particular order, just picking them up and jamming them back into that liner two and three at a time. No hurry at all now, just two or three in his left hand, then half a dozen in his right, whap, back down in the Styrofoam. Church ladies getting closer and closer, El getting in a groove with the flowers, me saying, "Give it up, man. It looks like a bomb went off in here. Looks like I peed in my pants for a year. You not understand what I'm saying? El, we gotta get outta town before . . ."

When the tall pruney one in the navy polka dot lurches around that door like something out of Mardi Gras hell croaking, "May we take just one teeny look before you bring it in?" And whatever was left in my bladder? Bam.

"We must be sure the colors are right," piped another one.

El took his hat off, having been raised in the Depression, and opened the door all the way.

"Oh my wooorrrd!" said the third lady.

"Oh my," echoed the second lady.

"It's gorgeous. I believe it's the most beautiful piece we've ever had. I'm going to call Irene as soon as we get it inside."

And there you go.

We spent thirty minutes turning and centering and adjusting that avant garde train wreck on the high altar of Presbyterianism, me dripping blue preservative water, and them thinking it was beautiful, and

El and me together finishing the hospital run before six-thirty. He had that kind of luck.

And for a time I did too.

During that same storm he said I got to go check she might've hurt herself, and I said she works in a bank for God's sake, what're you afraid happened, a paper cut? But he drove home anyhow, I mean the little house on Doster Street, and there she was, Patsy, alone in the bedroom her hand bleeding real bad and the mirror busted, with it wrapped in one of those ladies' handkerchiefs that won't soak up a thing. I said what are you doing home in the middle of the afternoon anyway while she stared into that hot dark stillness. I didn't feel well she said there's something wrong that feels twisted inside of me and just, Chad, please stay here while he fixes the fuses, just hold me until the lights come on. But your hand I said although she was warm and moist and her hair like roses but your hand. Will be all right she said if you just hold me. And so I did thinking that I was just holding her until the lights came on.

Elrod looked like a potato. Wore a gray fedora summer and winter, sweeping it off and crushing it against his heart on every occasion that demanded politeness, which, to his southern mind, was about every fifteen minutes. Black leather shoes that he never polished. Hawaiian shirts whenever he could. Pleated pants. White socks. Gray suit and bow tie for church. He had a nose that'd been broken enough times that you wondered what he did before you met him.

He spent his entire life looking for clues.

"Like my name," he said. "It ain't normal. Why would anybody call me that?"

It amazed him, his name did, and he printed it over and over in a blue notebook that he kept in the utility drawer of his worktable there at the flower shop. Along with a glass doorknob, a picture of his wife Patsy, broken watches, rubber bands, everything electrical that he could lay his hands on. And keys, hell yeah, maybe a hundred of them on a wire loop all worn smooth and forgotten. He just collected stuff. Sometimes he'd go looking for the one item he needed, just pick himself up and go, wham like that, maybe returning after lunch with a burned-out fuse, thinking.

Other days he might hit the brakes so hard it would stop time—you had to be ready for this—and he'd descend into the traffic to rescue a left-handed glove, a cracked mirror, a ribbon, a radio antenna. He cleaned and saved these things, arranged and rearranged his drawer, packed items away in those little boxes that cans of spray paint came in. Write in his notebook. Why should I care? He would let me drive as soon as we hit the city limits, on account of driving made him nervous. Or maybe distracted him from the search that eventually became his life.

Like the time we were five miles out on a dirt road that'd just been laid quiet by one of those summer storms. Searching for something—I don't remember really, one of those rural cemeteries maybe or a mailbox number—anyhow something that we weren't finding—so that we're just cruising, sort of lost in the warm, damp reordering of the world. And then there, on the other side of the windshield, at no particular distance from us, was a perfectly circular rainbow. For real. I didn't know the things existed.

I say, "Good God A'mighty, do you see that?" But of course he's been watching longer than I have; and who, besides El, could keep perfectly still and perfectly quiet inside of a miracle?

"You can't close it up like that," I insist. "You can't make no bull's-eye out of a rainbow."

"Sometimes you can," whispers Elrod Weiss.

Pretty soon I've got my head out of the driver's side window, squinting, one hand on the wheel, because for a moment it does seem like there's a figure in the center of the thing, the face of someone I might recognize. The air finally turning pure and cold in the after breeze, but I'm shivering from something else, and he's saying, "Patsy. That's my Patsy all up there in the yellow and blue. And pink. You see that? That's who it is." Not even surprised. "Better let me drive now; it's a rainbow here but a cloud over Morton, and she gets afraid." Though his hands didn't shake a bit.

Before Irene took him in, he drove a water truck for the county, one of those big tankers that sprinkles down the dust on gravel roads or washes dirt and trash off the regular highways. Big yellow boy with one of those black-and-white license tags saying "Bladen County—Permanent" like it was a monument or something. And thank God he didn't smoke and had a sister who could offer him a job when, you know, times got bad.

Because once he wheeled into Bub's Esso, said to the new guy fill her up, and headed off to visit Patsy during his lunch hour, before they were married I guess. And the new guy's yelling after him, "Filler up? Filler up? That mother holds five thousand gallon." Which would have turned a normal human being around, suggesting, as it did, frightening possibilities; but we're talking about Elrod Weiss here, who didn't veer one degree off course for anybody, yelling back, "Dus put it on the county ticket."

Well, that's what the kid does, because this is NASCAR country and, hell, anybody might need five thousand gallons of high-octane racing fuel. So it must have taken the whole hour to fill that tank until it was sloshing over the hatch and smelling like whiskey. Then here comes El back from lunch or whatever, hops in, and heads out to the bypass for his first run of the afternoon.

Okay, gets out to the new bridge, kicks on his sprayers just like always, and starts washing down the pavement with the highway equivalent of lighter fluid. He can't smell a thing, you know, on account of the busted nose, and he can't hear anything either on account of the radio. And he can't see anything either—like the road crew diving left and right—on account of he's in a groove now washing all that crap away like it was cheap sin. Pretty soon there're little rivers of gasoline.

Then the port-a-john gets deodorized. And maybe a few guys have their pants hosed down when they're too slow in vaulting for cover. But no more damage than that: God is watching over him just like always. So he drains the tank all the way down to empty over a three-and-a-half-mile straightaway without dropping a match, scratching a gravel spark, or backfiring. Then, same as always, he turns off the highway and heads back into town for another fill-up. Simple as that.

Which is when the far flagman starts sniffing and the site supervisor starts bellowing, "S'going on down there?" and the fellas wave their arms and yell back but don't come far out of the bushes. And the supervisor goes purple in the face howling at the flagman and the others, "You bastids wanna get fired? You think this is communis' Russia, you can take a corporate rest period?" Staggerwalking down the embankment at about the same time that the flagman clambers over the side of the half-built bridge that's sticking out into nowhere, figuring he needs to get his cigar going again in order to establish his full transportation department authority, and lights up.

It's like he lived a charmed life.

I told her I really did I said you think I don't know you're probably faking just to get attention. God knows you've got Daddy and Aunt Lib wrapped around your little finger and now you want to be my mamma too well you can forget it. I'm hanging around with whoever I want to hang around with okay because it's maybe all right to smile every once in a while and enjoy life instead of being you. We're not twins, not really, I mean is there a boy in the entire school who's ever touched you? I don't see how you can stand yourself I really don't you're such a faker. You think I don't know what you're doing in there, your own sister doesn't know, running to the bathroom every time so they won't think you're such a cow with that fake cough oh please. It's like you're being so pure you can't defile yourself with food or whatever, like you're the virgin bride or something, and then you think you can just preach to me like that? Let me tell you something pretty baby you ought to look in a mir-

*ror sometime. You are a cow. And if you want to starve yourself to death
that's fine with me.*

Every once in a while we'd pass a blur on the side of the road, and
he might say tomato can or dead dog or chain gang, like they were
all parts of the same puzzle, which if he twisted and turned just right
would all at once fit together. A week might go by and then he'd say,
"Remember that tomato can?" Like it didn't make any difference as to
who was hearing him.

And one of the yahoos down at Bub's would say, "Damaters?"

"Yeah. Del Monte or Heinz?"

Guy would shrug, wink at the others, say, "Del Monte. Del
Montier'n hell."

And this would be enough to send him into a trance, cleaning his
ear with a toothpick, thinking, until maybe the one piece of information would fit with another piece that he'd saved for months. Squinting
this time at me, "That a fig tree or a 'simmon tree we hit over to the
War Memorial?"

I'd say, "Fig."

Then he'd narrow his eyes some more—"That's what I thought."

Of course the lady designers who worked in the back of the flower
shop never understood. The atmosphere was too dense. Back there a
sort of chemical fog hung over everything. I hated the time we had to
work inside. Inside the shop he was just another man, a drudge like
those who worked the denim plant, breathing the same poisons, scur-
rying back and forth to do as he was told. Preservatives, dyes, glues,
fungicides, spray paints, disinfectants floating everywhere. It was like a
flower factory. I remember this clearly.

There were rules. Chrysanthemums got a shot of hair spray to keep
them from shattering, or sometimes you dripped candle wax on the
backs of the petals. Carnations got dipped in vinegar dye. Leaf-Cote
made the greenery shine on Tuesdays and Saturdays; it smelled like
varnish and alcohol. And long-stemmed roses—you already know

this—are bred purely for color and tight buds. They take their scent from chloral benzoate and artificial perfumes. Even today. And snapdragons have got no scent at all. Gladiolus get sliced on the diagonal, the stems soaked in a solution of soda ash to keep the blossoms from wilting. While orchids get snipped and inserted into little syringes of water, taped down into their boxes like they're on life support. So that after a while nobody has to teach you the one thing that stays with you through the years—that all these flowers are dead.

So what is it that you smell? I mean that musky sweet summer greenhouse scent wafting out into the showroom that makes you wish you could take it home in a spray can, that smell? I'll tell you what it is. It's stripped leaves. Wilted baby's breath. Browned petals. Stem ends, brittle galax, dried lycopodium, dead ferns. Tons of Spanish moss that they use as packing material. Garbage. You can sweep and empty four times a day and there's still a residue, a green, mosslike stain in the linoleum. It's pollen and crushed stems. Dried rosebuds that have fallen beneath the tables. Old water. It smells sweet, the whole of it, like the perfume of some lost Eden. And it stays sweet in your memory, the way flowers ought to be, until you know.

That's what you smell.

They moved to Morton oh I don't know 'bout ten, twelve years ago that's when Ed joined the Rotary and all but, no, it's not like I knew 'em real well. Had the one daughter a course and she lived at home and I mean boy she was a knockout you know what I mean? I mean a real knockout. Came there one time to pick up Ed when he was still attending and I'm in the living room waiting you know looking at all these pictures they got on the piano in the shelves and everywhere like they got stock in Kodak or something. And she comes through, Patsy does, and you couldn't help but make the connection. I mean hell I was just talking that's what I do for a living I sell things. Cars. And she said no that's my sister Clare she was killed in an accident. Just like that like she'd done give all the sorrow and tears she had to give and just didn't have any energy anymore. I

mean Jesus like she was making conversation or something and you got
to figure a car accident right so what could I say? Hell, mister, I wouldn't
hurt anybody for love nor money I mean just standing there like that,
what could I say? I never counted on twins.

Once in the autumn I saw leaves falling from a sugar maple close to
our house. Some spiraling down, some blown by the first breath of
winter; and every one, as soon as it released its hold, would burst into
flames and hang in red-orange glory for a moment, like the sails of
pirate ships set ablaze. Anyhow—what I thought. Every single leaf, a
flame. A conflagration in every gust of wind. This really happened.

And there, standing in the street, waiting for El to pick me up, hoping for a whirlwind, I watched them fly. Flicker and flame. Catching
one and feeling the momentary sting before it turned to ash in my
hand. I still have the mark of it. And then he was there, the mirror
on the right side of the truck almost bumping my shoulder, and him
reaching across the seat and throwing open the door and saying, "You
better crawl in, boy. You better crawl in before they set your hair on
fire."

I'm not saying it was right and I'm not trying to make excuses or any-
thing I don't want you to think I'm a hypocrite. It was wrong okay? I
made peace with that a long time ago. It just wasn't as simple as you
think. I mean good God she dated a damn criminal for a year and then
turned around and married an ape what does that sound like to you? It
was like she wanted life to punish her or something, which you can't even
imagine with somebody that beautiful you know what I mean? There
were days at the bank she came in with cuts, bruises on her arms or face
when you just wanted to put your arm around her. She was so sad. Look
I don't even know what I'm saying anymore I just know I would have
done anything to make her smile for a second. I won't say I loved her
but I did in a way and I would have done anything. . . . And I'll tell you
something else I would have killed the son of a bitch if I'd thought he

was doing it to her. But maybe she was hurting herself, you know what I'm saying? There's just no way to tell if you ask me.

He was terrified of dead people. He hated funeral homes even though they were the first places in the South to be air-conditioned, and we always made the cemetery run around noon just to be sure that we weren't overtaken by nightfall, but here's the funny thing. He knew the location of every grave in maybe two dozen cemeteries. Like he had a personal relationship with every corpse in Bladen County.

El never touched a casket. Never looked upon a body if it was in an open coffin. Never spoke in a room where there was a corpse, I don't know, maybe because he was holding his breath, I just don't know. And always he washed his hands after handling funeral flowers. Always. Used a big yellow bottle of Joy back there at the utility sink.

We had to go to Payne & Pinkerton one time, the colored funeral home there in Morton that took up three floors of a colossal white house on Houston Street, looked like a plantation. And the guest of honor was this fat lady, member of the Eastern Star or something, who just barely fit into her casket, which looked like a double-wide to me. They must have tucked her in with a crowbar and a shoehorn. Anyway, she's laying there sweet and serene as can be in a pink chiffon dress, white gloves, your pearl earrings, pearl necklace, and all your Eastern Star secret paraphernalia—except for one thing—the pink and white corsage that we've got to pin on her just before the service.

So what do you think, I'm going to do it? I'm fourteen years old and this involved touching a dead lady's breast in a colored funeral home that looked like Tara on an oiled-up dirt road where no sane white person would go after six o'clock on a Saturday night knowing that Roosevelt was no longer a favored name among Negro parents. What am I trying to say? I'm saying the times they were a changing, and you didn't want to handicap your future by maybe getting killed over some aspect of the new social order that you hadn't figured out yet. So I said, "Just leave the box on the front pew or give it to the oldest daughter, man, but let's hit the road before they bring in the forklift and she tips it over on one of us."

But no.

He had to do it. Take away everything else, and that's what was left. A gentleman. I can see his hands shaking to this day. See him swallowing hard. Taking that corsage up in one hand, the pin in the other, working his way up to the casket with slow shuffling steps. Till it gradually occurred to me what he was going to do as he took the pin. Eased it through the center of the bottom carnation until it stuck out the other side about an inch and a half. Then—whap—straight into her like a thumbtack.

Except I'm the one who squealed. "Oh God, no! What'd you do that for, man?! Jeezus Christ, El, you think they don't shoot to kill down here?"

"We got to go," is all he said. "It's after four."

"You got that right! Grab your hat, we gotta haul ass before the Fruit of Islam comes pouring through that door. Head for the border, you moron!" Just as she came in—all dressed in white—this younger version of the poor lady in the coffin, weeping.

She said El you think we could have stewed tomatoes tonight? I thought I saw a can of stewed tomatoes in the cabinet.

And now there is only one thing left, so I will tell it.

Patsy Burdette had long auburn hair and epilepsy. By the time she was thirty, I guess, she was working in the Morton Federal Savings and Loan, and I worshiped her. So did El. She painted her toenails, which you could see in the summer whenever she wore sandals, and never a piece of jewelry anywhere except the rings that El bought her when they were married, long before I started to work at Weiss Florist. And he was faithful as a dog. Never mind the rumors, he drove home for lunch every day so they could see each other for a few extra minutes. Sometimes there'd be guests, sometimes not.

He'd call Patsy every day to be sure she'd taken her medicine. We could be out delivering on the other side of the moon, and he'd pull in to some little country store and ask to use the phone, holding it out away from his ear like this because he had hearing like a bat, sort of talk into the mouthpiece like it was a microphone. You could hear her tiny voice on the other end saying, "What? Who is this? El, is that you? Who is this?"

And every Saturday I'd go with him, you know, to lunch at their house, an unpainted bungalow on Doster Street with a gravel driveway sounded like you were driving over crackers until you pulled up in the carport, and there she'd be, so happy to see us. And maybe one of her friends from the bank inside having lunch too, also happy to see us. El did almost all the housework; the place looked like a dollhouse, fussy clean, I guess on account of where she lived before they were married.

Then she died in December the year before I went away to college. He just cruised in one evening, maybe later than usual, maybe after drinking a little, nobody knows for sure; I just remember people talking. Anyway he went home for supper to the house with the dark shutters and low-hanging pines and found her in the bathtub. She'd had a seizure, the long auburn hair floating in arabesques upon the surface of the water, perfectly serene and beautiful. He loved her so. Laid her out in the bed before the ambulance got there, in a satin nightgown, covers up to her neck, the thick silky hair brushed and dried, arranged in waves down to her shoulders. No one knows how he did it.

So now I'm one of them I guess I don't know what happened I just turned around took my eyes off him for a second changed my clothes and there you were my own son. But I can tell you this much no matter what they say this is a love story for your mother yes but also for you. Because when he finally slammed that battered door of the old panel truck and the looming echo faded and we had made the last hospital run of the day it was no longer the spring of 1965 and now I have to strain to get him back. He was Elrod Weiss. The funniest man I ever knew.

THE TICKING AND TOCKING
OF THEIR HEARTS

Cutters

EMILY

Thinks this might be the cover shot. Straight down the path with a very wide-angle lens. Which, of course, will yield some distortion near the edges. But she doesn't care. In fact she hopes that the overhanging branches will print like a blurry hand thrown up in front of a face. It's the flat white facade of their church that she really wants to show—a picture-postcard set on the edge of their world. Like you could step around that clapboard corner and fall straight into hell. That's what Sam can't understand.

He thinks they've come for the story. She thinks they've come for the girl.

So Emily tightens the legs of the tripod and checks depth of field while they wait for the families.

SAM

Sits on a gray boulder for most of the morning, inhaling one cigarette after another and pretending to study his notepad. White pages go fluttering in the wind like a magician's dove. Every now and then he jots a question and stares at the next mountain as if searching for an answer. The boulder fits him like a throne, and it has a lichen-covered ledge that he can use as an armrest and a vague comfort that sends him musing. "So. You think they'll actually bring the kid?"

Emily doesn't rise out of her crouch or turn her head when she answers. "It's her father. Of course they'll bring her."

"Great."

"I doubt they trust us very much. Would you?"

"I doubt they ever saw the picture in the first place. They probably aren't big newspaper readers up here. And besides—that was two years ago."

"They saw it. Everybody in the country saw it. So how about bringing me that battery pack from the Jeep."

"I should have been a lawyer," Sam says.

"You should have been a reporter." Emily takes a few more test shots with the Polaroid and listens for the crunch of tires on gravel.

"I'm just saying you can't make a story out of an obit notice."

"So leave. I'll handle it."

"I think maybe you don't remember who we're dealing with here."

"Right. They take up serpents. It almost slipped my mind."

"You're not going to save her, Emily, and she's not going to love you for trying."

"I think maybe you're right. Now how about hooking up that hose and giving me a fine spray over the front of the whole thing. Okay?"

EMILY

Loves the look he gives her; but this time he lumbers away, untangling the stiff hose and finally throwing up a wide fan of water. She wants a mist but even a torrent will do—an old photographer's trick that seems to work, coalescing light around the window frames. She runs a roll through the Pentax and hopes for magic.

"They're going to come crackling down that road any minute," Sam yells. "And see what? Mrs. Greenburg's son with his thumb over the end of a hose watering their church."

Emily can't tell if his hand is shaking or if it's simply the way he sprays the water. She feels a warm current of air that has been rising from the valley all morning, as if the mountain thinks it can take back summer. And there's a faint scent of bread and apples from somewhere below. At last the sun drops low enough to transform the windows into dead eyes, the door into a gaping mouth, the steeple into a tall dunce cap. The wet paint turns a leaden white. It is what she has wanted most, the image of a clown face upon black velvet.

After she finishes shooting, Emily carries the tripod back to the Jeep and contemplates the almost invisible road that brought them to this place two years ago. It coils its wet way around the mountain and stretches back two years to when she and Dietz did their first story about the Holiness people. Since then she has not returned, which leaves her wondering if she will be remembered at all.

JARED

Tries to explain over lunch at his desk, egg salad dribbling over tomorrow's news. ". . . couple of years ago. So I sent her up to the same little town to cover the trial. Seems one of the saints wanted to eliminate his wife using a copperhead, so you figure that's got to be good for a feature story, right? Maybe a cover for the weekend magazine. Anyhow. I sent Emily and this kid named Dietz. Some hillbilly dumping ground up in the mountains. And I've got 'em camping out in a local motel, sending back dailies and taking in a few of the religious services. You know, the snake-handling stuff. Getting brotherly and sisterly with the families. Spending weekends with them at camp meeting or whatever the hell it is they do. Anyhow, developing trust. Next thing I hear, Emily's cut herself, sliced the shit out of her arm on some broken glass. And then, get this, one of the grandmas takes her in. Bandages her up. Prays over her night and day—who the hell knows? Then, bam, the trial's over. Just like that. The guy gets life, and we bang out a story from Dietz's notes. I put Sam on the rewrite, and we go with it on a Sunday. A month later one of Emily's pictures, the cover shot, gets nominated for a Pulitzer. Damnedest thing you ever saw in your life."

SAM

Spends the early afternoon on the side of the church where the drop-off is steep, setting up equipment, loading film, helping her shoot from impossible angles. Stringing wire for the lights while she pokes around in the basement. Conspiring, he thinks. Framing some guy for a crime he doesn't even know about yet. While all morning her eyes remain as empty as the space between stars. Where has she been, he wonders. Someone this beautiful, how can she hide?

And when they finally do arrive, the eight or ten silent families, they come like characters from a fairy tale, already ancient and unbelievable. Led by an old woman bent over her crooked cane. Followed by grave, silent children who hold hands. And two young mothers already pregnant beneath faded print dresses. Emily mingling easily among the women, Sam standing apart from the men, who appear to have been drawn in charcoal with brief, impulsive strokes. A tall teenager gives Emily a wiggle-fingered wave, and Sam wonders if she is the one. Tries to remember the picture of Marla Ann Creecy. Then tries adding two years.

The prelude is like any funeral, solemn and self-conscious—a touch to the shoulder, a whispered word or two as people file through the door; but the service itself opens with the first hint of guitar music and a sudden shout of praise. Emily takes his arm, and they fall into line behind an angular blond boy of maybe sixteen. At the threshold she slips her hand into his and draws him momentarily closer. "This," she promises, "is going to be the most erotic experience of your life. Trust me."

There is music already and singing, an "undeniable hypnotic appeal" that he will mention in the article. Maybe he will even call it the "little white church where they practice the only religion that's illegal in America." Toss in a few ironies, a few descriptive details. Three or four paragraphs if he ignores the extraneous stuff, like the stiff plastic bandages. Where Emily cut her fingers this morning. On the rocks by the basement door.

JARED

Gives Michael time to remember the picture, a close-up of a timber rattlesnake and the daughter of one of their preachers, Byron Creecy. Then he recalls for himself the girl, maybe twelve or thirteen years old, but not a day over that. "She's beautiful," he mutters. "Hair pulled back. Skin as smooth as cream. And got to be wearing her first touch of lipstick, which you notice immediately because of the natural contrast with the thing she's holding in her hands. And I mean, they're just about face to face. It's sickening the first time you see it, but you keep turning back to it as you read the story, like you can't believe the words without the help of the picture. So you look again, and she's still lifting him up like this, like an offering or something. Bastard's thicker than a man's arm, and the skin is splitting, flaking off in places, I don't know, maybe it's the time of year for them to molt or something, but it looks like he's being born right there in her hands. You can see the underbelly just emerging from the old skin, and it's not white like you'd expect. It's the color of melted gold. And the dead skin is like paper. But that's not what haunts you. I mean, the snake, that's not what stays with you when you close your eyes. It's the girl. That's what got this picture reprinted a million times. Her face. It's tilted a little to the side and back, her own eyes closed like she's in a trance, lips slightly parted, maybe praying. Emily told me they call it an Anointing, when the Holy Spirit descends on them and for a time they are invulnerable to poison or the sting of serpents or any mortal harm. Who the hell knows? I'm just telling you that's not what it looks like to me. Not like praying. I mean, you and I could wait a lifetime and still not get that shot. I'm just telling you what I remember. Because what it looks like to me is a first kiss."

BROTHER PAUL

Swings himself to his toes with each exclamation, arms pumping like pistons. As he says, "I know some people will say to you that Brother Byron must have been crazy, a sort of throwback to olden times. And

I do believe they were right. He was plumb Bible crazy and so sure in the Word that he gave himself up entire to the love of Jesus Christ with signs following. Because why? Because he understood this one plain spiritual fact: if there ain't nothing dangerous about your religion, then you might as well join a country club. If you ain't alive to the Spirit, then you might as well be dead to everything else. That's what I'm saying. You got to risk something—I'm telling you here today—when you stand before Almighty God. You got to be like old Moses on the mount stepping into the devouring fire of His presence, amen, and kept alive by nothing but his grace. And just because you're bathed in the Light don't mean you're going to live through it, my friend, I'll tell you that much. Oh, yes, and I'll tell you this too. I'd rather be snakebit than deaf to the Word a God."

SAM

Studies the face and finds a visible longing that the preacher cannot articulate. Sees Brother Paul praying at the lectern, stumbling through his litany of sins confessed and blessings conferred without hint of order or, perhaps, even understanding that the words should make sense. The prayer becomes a kind of chant, and the face, Sam sees finally, has become the meaning behind the prayer. It is a face filled with fear and desperate longing. And it is what Emily has brought him to see.

Sam finally shuts out the chaotic sounds and studies the other faces around him, finding the same plea. On an old man with stick-thin arms, a farmer perhaps, worn down by rock-filled fields. On a young woman, heavily pregnant and sitting alone. And on all the others. The forgotten faces of middle children of large families, who would do anything to be loved, faces fearful of being left behind, desperate for attention, pleading past all reason, "Please God. Look at me."

And after a time Byron Creecy is no longer a presence at his own funeral. There is simply a succession of readings, hymns, and reminiscences that, like the movements of a symphony, build to climaxes and then fall away into interludes of soft meditation offered by the guitar and keyboard. It is like the ebb and flow of the ocean that most of them have never seen. And it is more than an hour after the last mention of Brother Byron's name that the real moment arrives, a moment in the midst of a quiet hymn whose calm is broken by a shout.

The Spirit has descended upon a young man in the second pew, his body jerked into the aisle and made to shudder uncontrollably as a stream of babble pours from his mouth. Brother Paul makes room at the lectern, but the boy begins leaping like a man on a trampoline while several of the women start to clap and praise in their own tongues, reaching out from time to time like bathers about to step into a waterfall. The musicians increase the tempo as others stand and clap. The young mother hugging her belly and rocking as if soothing her just-born child. Sam looks over the whole room and gradually understands. That he and Emily are utterly alone. Wild music lifts them into the Anointing.

It's then that Sam notices her, the girl from the picture. She is looking back, studying him from a calm distance. The innocent eyes and pouting lips of a child, but someone too who is much older than the image in his mind. She is Marla Ann Creecy, the girl who waved to Emily and the reason that they are here.

Her black knit dress is her only hint of mourning, and her own face is unreadable as she sways with the music, moving more like a practiced dancer than someone who has been seized by the Spirit. She watches Sam and Emily with open intensity, the way children examine strangers. And lets them watch her. Her sweater falls away, and she seems to leave the present with ease, surrendering to some rhythm older than the law of Moses.

She dances, and Sam watches with his story-mind and something more. Because her breasts are as full and round as a woman's, and the dress follows her waist like a second skin, flowing over her hips and falling loosely to her knees. With her arms outstretched now and her face turned aside, she becomes in black and gold the renewed image from the picture; and when the music dies, she sinks into a convenient pew, lifts her face to the rafters, and draws a lover's deep sigh.

"We've got to talk to her," Emily says. "When this is over, we've got to get to her. Alone."

Sam blinks, and it is Emily, whose eyes are filled with fire.

JARED

Looks up at Michael, then back at his sandwich. After two more bites he makes a tight ball of tissue, dropping it into the Styrofoam cup, which, in turn, he drops into the trash. Running his tongue over his teeth and ruminating. "Marla Ann Creecy is a minor. And both her parents are dead, that's true. But there's not going to be another custody hearing because the laws of our great state have already provided that she live with her grandparents, who just happen to reside in another century." Jared looks up again to see if this announcement has had any effect. "So why am I telling you what you might already know? Because Emily takes pictures, Michael. She makes things happen, you know what I mean? Dangerous things. I just thought you'd want to talk to her." He waits, scratches an eyebrow. "Because we got a saying in this business. 'Every story is two stories.' You know what I mean?"

MICHAEL

Remembers a motel room as cold and filthy as the creek itself.

He and Emily are still twins, still so close that they don't yet think of themselves as separate people. They are eight years old, and it is summer, and the sinuous water has worked its magic, tempting them away from the tepid motel pool, down to the long embankment, and into the writhing current beneath the trees. Where they play for hours. Building the dam, bathing in mud, and searching for treasure among piles of trash. Without one thought of danger. Until the sun sinks low enough to throw a shadow over neverland and they go running up the path, flecks of grass sticking to their ankles. Then grit from the parking lot. Then the hot exhaust of the air conditioner just as they reach the door. And he remembers plunging into the room without thinking that there might be broken glass, rusty cans, twisted wire just beneath the surface of things. But it's only Mother and the man sitting on the edge of the bed. And they are twins who've come dripping from the creek as it closes over them, the dark liquid cold of that particular afternoon.

Inside the room there are crumpled food wrappers on the carpet like paper boats. A pizza box yawning and sweaty cups. But most of all there's Emily, one step ahead of him because she didn't stop and look in the parking lot. Who's got the shower going before he can step out of his bathing suit, before Mother can finish saying, "Put them in the sink and run water on them. And rinse them out good." Words that get lost in the clutter. So that when he steps behind the pink plastic curtain there is nothing but thunderous warmth and Emily with her hands above her head redirecting the spray into the flimsy metal walls. She twirls and dances and squeals. He wrenches the knobs so the water goes cold and hot and cold again until they are covered with goose bumps and giggling and collapsing against the rusty seams of the cabinet. They are twins. Sleek and brown as otters. Splashing and shoving. Thin glistening versions of the same person, except for the tight flesh between his legs and the smooth white cleft between hers.

It is the last few moments of their last afternoon as twins. The last secret telling and touching of their one life. In the aftermath of what happens next she will become Emily, and he will become Michael, and they will reenact this pain for years. Of course it is an accident. He simply slips. And in the instant between standing and falling, he steps onto the slotted metal grate that covers the drain, where the ragged edge of one corner slices through his sole like a filleting knife. Though at first it is only a warm hint of what is to come. Then, after he falls, a twisty stream of red begins running into the drain. It works its way from his foot, across the dimpling shower floor, and through the green-rusted slots. And then he screams.

There are hands that lift him, strong arms that scoop him up and wrap him in the one damp towel and plop him on the stranger's lap. Their mother's growing panic. Then the deep voice that settles their cold fear. "Better let me have a look at that, Chief. You might gonna need stitches." His hand is as big as Michael's shoe, and when he clamps the foot closed, there is only a thin trickle between his fingers—and after another minute only a dull ache. Even before their mother returns with more towels and antiseptic, even before they bundle him into the car and carry him into the emergency room, where the indifferent resident will set the stitches, he knows he is safe. That he has been gathered up by a man who can crush pain with one hand, and Michael knows without a doubt that this will be the best day of his life.

Though not for the sister who stands shivering.

She is small and cold, pale with the certainty that the blood will never stop. Even when their mother returns. Even when Michael begins to howl anew, she keeps her distance. Michael sees her step back to the wall, slide down into a squat, both hands between her legs. Her hair still streaming icy-clear rivulets. She is like an orphan lost in the snow. And he is like the boy in the warm cottage, looking out. At least that is what he remembers. Because it's who he is today.

EMILY

Recites the same history to each new therapist, a narrative that has been reduced over time to formula, an incantation of sorts whose individual words mean nothing. "I was eleven or twelve," she begins, "walking with a group of girls across an asphalt parking lot where I found the first one, a bright piece of broken glass, yellow and curved like a scythe, that a magpie might pick up, or a child. And that is the one that I used to draw the first red scream across my wrist. So they told their mothers that I had tried to commit suicide, as if anyone who wanted to kill herself would do that and laugh, though of course the cure was the same.

"And this is what I said to Michael the summer after he graduated from medical school. 'What if you had bees inside of you? What if you had swallowed them somehow and they were carpenter bees working away inside the wooden you? What if you had soaked up poison like a sponge, so that it went flowing not through your veins but through the crooks and cavities of your flesh, all through your secret self? Would you try to get it out?'

"Because it's not a matter of pain. There isn't any. It is a relief. I can't explain more than that. See? A crisscross of white lines. I can read them like a map."

SAM

Swears a photographer told him this. That if you stare intently at the horizon during the last minutes of daylight you can see a brilliant flash of green just as the sun disappears. A green explosion, lasting for maybe a tenth of a second, right along the razor's edge of earth and sky. He thinks about asking Emily, but Emily is still up at the church talking to the girl's grandparents, something about giving her a ride home. And Sam decides to look for himself. It's what he's doing while he waits for Marla Ann Creecy.

From the rocky ledge where he is standing, the church looks like a small white storage shed in the midst of a pasture, and the view out over the valley is worth an entire book of photographs. For a moment Sam thinks that the Holiness people are not only fugitives from civilization but also profoundly wise. Then hears the clatter along the trail behind him. Someone calling attention to herself before she arrives. And stepping next to him as if they'd known each other all their lives.

"Emily says you all can give me a ride home in the Jeep."

"Yeah. We'd just like to talk to you for a few minutes. If that's okay."

"Sure. She was up here a couple of years ago. Everybody knows her, and they don't mind."

"Good. Good, I, uh . . . I'm not the same guy she was with last time."

"I know. I bet we seem pretty different to you, don't we?"

"A little bit. Maybe we could talk about it. Get a hamburger or something."

The sun sets, and he sees nothing. Only her green eyes that have been with him since the service. When he finally does turn around, Emily is still nowhere in sight, and Marla Ann is not the person he thought she was. She is far too old.

"I've got something you want to see," she whispers; it is a new tone, low and conspiratorial. "Up at the church. In the basement." And she is suddenly a child again who can't keep a secret.

"Really? Where's Emily?"

"Up there. Waiting for us."

And so he follows, knowing already that the story has taken a new twist. That Emily isn't just waiting. In fact is nowhere in sight. And the last car is disappearing down the misty road to town.

"Where's your Jeep?" the girl asks.

"We parked it a little off the road. So the rest of you could get through."

"Oh. You ever been to a Holiness church before?"

But since his lips are dry, he simply shakes his head.

The basement is like a shallow grave beneath the church, its door almost level with the ground because the slope is steep. They go down two steps, then down another as they cross the threshold into a damp well of earth.

There are cardboard boxes disintegrating into the floor. Tightly tied stacks of newspaper. A whole pew shoved up against sagging book-shelves. A lawn mower. And enough tools and paintbrushes, rolls of wire, to suggest the innocent accumulation of any barn or attic. Except for the broken gravestone and the expression on Marla Ann's face. She glows with anticipation, knowing that there is a sweet secret only she can reveal, like a girl who sneaks her boyfriend into her bedroom for the first time. She steps back and invites him to look closer before showing the thing itself, the real reason she has brought him here. And he is a man who cannot take his eyes away, even though he knows that there will not be a happy ending.

So he does as she wills him. He plays the game. Finding first a glass tea jar holding perhaps half a gallon of filthy, swamp-colored water and then beside it, on the same shelf, a hatchet and a can of gasoline. Higher up there is an old photograph album that, at first, he believes is what she wants him to find. But when he reaches, she is suddenly there beside him, murmuring, "No. Lower. Go back to where you were." Squatting beside the shelves, chin on her knees now. Smiling. When he kneels, she draws in the long deep breath of calm certainty.

It is the jar she wants him to see. He looks. And the water moves.

It is a liquid thing inside the jar, but not the muddied water that he thought. It is coiled upon itself in multicolored brown and black and gold, breathing so subtly that it looks like the rocking of pond water after a pebble has been dropped in, its head submerged among the rippling scales. A body swelling and constricting in easy slumber.

"They just got him," she says. "He's never been in church before."

Sam can't move. "Why did you bring me here? Why would you . . . ?"

But she reaches past him, brushing his cheek with her arm, and taps the side of the jar. Inside, the familiar shape rises up from the tight coils, black tongue flickering. "Shhh," she says. "There's nothing to be afraid of." Lifting the jar now with both hands and holding it next to her own cheek, giving just the slightest shake until the tail stands up and makes the first tentative vibrations. "You're safe with me," she says. "You're safe." In hypnotic repetition. Until the open mouth of the vessel is before him, and she is saying, "Touch it."

The words should come like an electric shock, but they are numb and distant.

"That's what you have to do," she says. "Touch it. If you want to feel what I feel."

Sam's hand moves through the thick air. Across the open mouth of the jar. And down, into the perfect moment, when it happens. There is a flash of light, a whir of advancing film, and then an explosion of glass. His eyes blink shut, but not before he sees the green aurora at the edge of her world.

MICHAEL

Loves his sister. She will call him once or twice a year with her overpowering need. Can you meet me, she will ask, in the aftermath of a story about a shooting or a stabbing or a fire. Can you meet me in the parking lot of some cheap motel, her voice as faint as a child's, and hold me, Michael, long enough to stop the shaking. Could you meet me? Michael? At the foot of a mountain where two highways cross. And bring your bag.

Breaker

So many times it seems eternal. She whines. I lie. It's our fate. We'll
be bound to each other in hell by tangled telephone lines, except this
time she reaches me through the air, across an entire ocean, inside an
airport terminal. It's like a wasp buzzing in my briefcase, and I extract
it with the tips of my fingers, holding the sound as close to my face
as I can bear. When I hear her voice, I realize that she can reach me
anywhere.

She says, without greeting, "Charles, I need a favor."

"You'll have to speak up," I tell her. "I don't think we have a good
connection."

"Charles, don't start. I need you to take Eric this weekend."

"Narissa? Is that you?"

"Anthony and I are doing a wedding upstate. I need you to take
Eric. Camping or something, you're always promising to take him
camping."

"Gee, Nariss, I'd love to help you, but I'm sort of tied up at the moment."

"Where are you?"

"Where am I?"

"Yes, Charles. Where. Are. You."

"You mean right now? Right this minute?"

"Charles, for God's sake!"

"Oh. Yeah, well, right now I'm in Marseilles. Might not be back for a while."

"You're in Marseilles?"

"Yeah. I do international maritime law, Narissa. You know, boats and water. This is a very logical place. You and Anthony ought to try it sometime."

"You're lying."

"You dialed the number."

I have a talent for finding the argument-stopper. It's a gift—knowing that she had got the maid to call my office and then dial this number before touching the phone herself. And also knowing she would never admit it.

The truth is that I was in Marseilles yesterday, where they sell cold medication at the airport shops. Today I am here, with a sinus infection, at another airport on an island whose name I have forgotten, just off the coast of Liberia. Barely able to breathe. Right now I am waiting for a man named Robert N'mburo, who is a local chieftain, or whatever they call them over here, hoping that he will be able to write his own name. He isn't really required to write his own name, but it would make this whole charade easier. So I pinch my nose. Take sips of air through my mouth. Then finally, at some point, look down and see that I really am fondling a cigarette.

Waiting, after I get rid of the phone call, the way you do in this section of Africa.

And what a dump.

I can say that because my employer—International Filth, Human Misery, and Contamination, Incorporated—owns everything in sight. Really. We own the airstrip, the island itself, approximately two hundred ships in various stages of disassembly, the trucks, the cables, the acetylene torches, the infirmary such as it is, the dead fish, the twenty-four miles of shoreline, and mineral rights. It's all in my briefcase, printed on $8\frac{1}{2} \times 14$ legal sheets. We own the dump and most of the human beings who live here. On the island at the end of the earth, whose name I cannot at present remember. And we own the terminal building in which I am sitting. And of course we own me, down to the pinstripes and New Orleans accent—slightly adulterated by the necessity of living in Manhattan for the past fourteen years and representing said ironies in federal district court from time to time.

So I'll say it again because these little moments don't last. And because I like saying it. We own this part of the world. We *are* the government. We are the parent, the tribal elder, the proprietor, and savior of this island. We are God, and this is our Earth. It is our lump of dirt until it outlasts its usefulness, a moment which, unfortunately, arrived about six weeks into our last business quarter. Paradise is still profitable, but when your legal liabilities—not to say the closing arguments of several lawsuits—begin to creep into the accounting. . . . Well, that's why I'm here. To shut it all down.

This particular building reminds me of a subway station, except that it has an oily teakwood floor and a few windows the size of portholes. Nevertheless, the air is subway air. I know it when I see it. And there's rust blossoming on the walls, like the mineral gardens in caves. I've never seen anything quite like it—great cankerous rust flowers, as crenellated as carnations, growing on the walls of a building. It's unnatural. Someone should pass an ordinance. The place smells like a fish market and echoes like a cathedral. I keep expecting someone to walk by and use the word *aeroplane*. That's the sort of thing that pops into my mind when I'm not thinking about the fact that I am seven hundred miles from the nearest aspirin. And the fact that no one in this room has ever heard of Robert N'mburo. And the further fact that my wristwatch is missing.

Someone should have shut this place down years ago.

Did I say International Filth, Misery, Etc.? I believe I meant to say International Recovery Systems, Inc., a Fortune 500 company of sterling reputation whose major concern at the moment is that I make those two hundred ship carcasses disappear. Before, of course, they generate further unfortunate publicity and a verdict or two.

The really interesting thing is that I can do it.

At least, I can make them disappear from my client's side of the table. As I said, I do not require Mr. Robert N'mburo's signature. I simply require evidence that my masters have made a good-faith effort to eliminate the atrocious conditions in which Mr. N'mburo's people labor, those impoverished shipbreaking members of his tribe who, as luck would have it, are also members of what might be the most dangerous profession on earth. Thank God they haven't yet discovered lawyers.

In any event, my name is Charles Metairie Allemand.

And it is my sincere belief that the only truly happy people in the world at this instant are the two little boys, as black as bear cubs, who have been roly-polying, climbing, and chasing each other through the one big room since we got off the plane together. Their mother is a dignified young woman who watches them, and me, with equal calm. And I watch them because they have just found the one oddity about this place that even sarcasm cannot explain. It is a large marine compass, of the kind they used to have on sailing vessels, which has been bolted to the floor near one of the windows. Twice as large as a fire hydrant and as shiny as a medallion. And here is the human hope for all of us. It is the universal and ineluctable fact that no two boys anywhere in the world will ask *why* there is a marine compass in an airport. They will simply run to it and climb like monkeys. They will strain to lift it from the floor. They will try to make the needle move. They will fiddle and finagle and go belly-polishing over every inch of brass until one of them has clambered to the top and thrown his arms up like a champion. That's what I like about this pair. They're not lawyers.

I wonder which of them has my watch.

You see, I understand that there is a terrible logic holding this island to the surface of the earth. Different rules and regulations. And I know that the next few hours, or the next few days, will pass like a dream and that it will be useless to pretend otherwise. Sooner or later someone will sign the documents in my briefcase, perhaps even someone named Robert N'mburo, after which I will deliver one set to the Interior Ministry in Monrovia and then board the next flight to any major city in North Africa. Whence I will fly to Paris. Pick up an aspirin or twelve. Then from Paris to New York, where I will be paid an absurd amount of money by my employer, International Recovery Systems, Incorporated, for making this place disappear.

It's amazing how we can manipulate reality. Ten minutes ago, when the phone rang in my briefcase, every person in this building stopped to listen. Every one of them heard me lie to a woman who was not my wife, for a reason that I cannot, even at this moment, explain.

"Where are you?" she said. Just a disembodied voice from very far away, like a conscience.

"Where am I?" I said. "Do you mean right now? Where am I right this minute?"

And the voice said, "Charles, for God's sake. We need . . ."

And I said Marseilles. "I'm in Marseilles."

While no one even blinked.

My greatest fear is of dying at sea. Of being swallowed by the ocean itself or by one of its creatures. I dream about it after watching the History Channel, those World War II sagas where they show submarine footage and the old fellows talk about what it's like to be torpedoed. I have nightmares of being trapped in the bowels of a sinking ship as the first foam rushes across the deck and steel doors go slamming and then I realize that outside my ever-constricting bubble there will be no one left aboard to hear the hammering of my fists. I think of that from time to time and how easily the sea erases any hint of our passage. All the old fellows who didn't make it onto television. And I think how, in the midst of the gray Atlantic, five hundred miles from the continental shelf, the largest vessels go down without a ripple, slowly spinning through the first hundred feet of filtered light as schools of halibut scatter and strings of kelp become tattered streamers on the coffin as it drops into that darker deep, beyond anything even remotely human.

Down, down to the places where sea dragons and skeletal, armor-plated worms wear their own luminescence and stare with mindless curiosity at our own white orbs, while—still descending—we drift far past the point where every breathing thing has already imploded and the bones have turned to jelly. Until at last we settle, the two of us, ship and self, into the sedimentary muck, which oozes like cold syrup through the one open hatch and down the vacant stair. Somewhere on the abyssal plain.

Or I think at times of drowning within sight of shore, drifting into some sharp crevice between brown rocks or floating facedown in a tidal pool like a tourist diver who's lost his mask and fins. Dying there and being inflated by my own pompous gasses, only to be punctured by an inquisitive crab so that I might become a holiday for the millions who feed from the bottom up, a bounteous plantation of limpets and filter feeders, a pink crust of coralline algae outlining my form like chalk marks at the scene of a crime. While the urchins rejoice. I, bobbing like a buoy until all my fat has been suctioned away and the blue-tentacled anemones have lost their sting. So that I sink into a kind of immortality among a constellation of starfish, my ribs pointing toward the sun like the fingers of the first astronomer. At the bottom of a deep, deep sky.

And just before the jellied tentacles, when our marriage was breaking up and Narissa and I thought we could cure everything with a flight to that other paradise, I saw the battleship *Arizona*. Spectacularly visible from the air, resting in less than twenty feet of water beneath a pane of wavy green glass. Turrets perfectly aligned, the familiar white memorial like a crown on a hoary head. From my tiny window I could detect a peculiar undersea motion that made the ship's outline indistinct—an unresisting ebb and flow of marine plants that carpeted *Arizona* as if to assert how thoroughly, even in this remote and shallow puddle, the ocean would reclaim its own. Think of it, a battleship consumed by plants, and you will understand why as we prepared to land I told Narissa that we would not be among the tourists dropping their wreaths. Because I had already sensed that within inches of the surface were the outstretched arms of 1,177 sailors, a thought that terrified me even at a distance of several miles. As she leaned across to gape.

And now all these images flood my mind as I contemplate the young man standing in front of me. I'm trying to comprehend his words. He speaks perfect English, which is, after all, the official language of Liberia, but simple comprehension is not the problem. Rather, it sounds as though he is saying, "I have come to take you to the ship." A message that complicates things, since I am sure he means one of the skeletal ships being consumed along the shore.

"Mr. N'mburo sent you, yes?" I say.

"Yes, yes. Robert. I will bring you directly to him. Everything is arranged. I hope you had a decent and comfortable flight."

He is stick thin and just under six feet, a boy really, whose face is less than twelve years old and whose white shirt is buttoned to the collar. Perhaps one of the Bassa people come down from the hinterland with his parents to make money in the shipbreaking trade. I do not care to explain to him the horrors I associate with ships, but neither do I intend to meet Robert N'mburo onboard one of the floating corpses at the edge of this island. "There has been a mistake," I say to him. "I am supposed to meet Mr. N'mburo here, at this place, now."

"A mistake with many apologies, Mr. Allemand, which most assuredly is being met with correction, as everything is now in order. I have transportation immediately outside."

"What is your name?"

"Call me Sammy, that is the easy way. I will drive you immediately to your arrangement."

The absurdity of being driven anywhere by a twelve-year-old does not occur to me; it's the other absurdity that tingles along my spine. "Sammy, there is no need for anyone to be on a ship. In fact, I'm here to close down the shipyard. As a protection, for the workers. It's already decided. This meeting with your representative is just a formality really. A signature is all that's required. There won't be any more ships."

"Yes, I will take you. It is immediately arranged. I am an utmost excellent driver with apologies for this slight change, although I must believe that there will be more ships."

For a moment a flicker of fear crosses Sammy's face, and I want to say to him of course there will be more ships. There will always be rotting horror and putrefaction. But what I say instead is "I need for Mr. N'mburo to be here."

"Here? At this ship?"

Now he has confused me, and I have to stand and start over. Several people have come to stand with me and to offer help in several dialects. "No," I say. "Not a ship. I need you to bring Robert N'mburo here. To sign papers only."

"Here?" Sammy says.

The people nod, and I nod. "Yes. Here."

"To *this* ship?"

Everyone looks at me.

I look at the rust on the walls. The oily teakwood floor. Then Sammy takes my hand and leads me outside, several dozen yards out onto the airstrip itself where we turn and look and see the whole of it—a silhouette that still reminds me of a terminal building at some small airport upon some New England coast. Although now of course the details bring out the truth. There is the horizontal stripe, faded but still visible, just beneath a terraced array of windows, some with wipers still attached. Stanchions like a row of unthreaded needles picketing the open deck. Boom and funnels at the aft. The twin flags of America and Liberia fluttering from the radio mast. It is the superstructure of a cargo vessel, cut at her traverses, and dragged by some Egyptian strength across the beach and to this level stretch of sand. The type of thing I have seen in this part of Africa before, a solution so practical in its conception and yet so insane in its execution that you had sooner believe that a ship had fallen from the sky, burying herself, like the *Arizona*, in a shallow grave.

The boy looks at the terminal building and then looks at me, smiling at the colossal joke. "I am thinking that you are finding this very hard to believe, the way things are done."

I feel like a man who's been lifted out of the grave, and for a moment I share his humor. "I don't find anything hard to believe, Sammy. For the right money . . . , I'll believe anything you say."

This is something he understands and that unleashes a flood of enthusiasm. "Gbambhala is a most logical place. We are not part of Liberia at all, Mr. Allemand, I am hoping you understand. The entire island has been purchased by the United States, and we are working for America."

I don't contradict him. "Gbambhala? Has it always been called that?"

"Yes, always I believe. And now you are still wishing to meet here?"

I stare toward the harbor, but all I can make out are wild sea oats and a scattering of palms and *bilinga*. The sun is low enough to make the beach road look like a strip of silver. "No. No, I just need a minute to, ah, get oriented here, Sammy. I just need to . . . get this over with and then . . . When did you say was the last flight, to the mainland?"

"There is a flight to Marrakech very late. Usually eleven o'clock or perhaps midnight. And a ferry boat to Abidjan across the water, in that direction perhaps a mile. Sometimes it arrives in the evening." He has a future, this kid who can remember more details than your average litigator.

"That's fine. Let's try to get me on that plane. But first let's make the call on Mr. N'mburo, wherever he happens to be."

There are only three places in the world where shipbreaking occurs on a large scale: Alang in India; Chittagong in Bangladesh; and the six-mile stretch of beach at Gbambhala—a wholly owned subsidiary of International Recovery Systems, Inc. There are no large shipbreaking operations anywhere in the Western Hemisphere. Only desperately poor people can afford this work, and only a government ruled by a lunatic would sell an island to a private shipbreaking firm. Still, it is one of the most profitable enterprises on earth. The turbines alone from a twenty-five-year-old tanker will fetch nearly a million dollars. The unburned fuel and oil, electrical equipment and wiring, wood furniture and decking will bring in another half million. Then you are down to the precious metals—brass, copper, and steel—so much steel that Chittagong supplies the entire steel output for Bangladesh. There is not another steel mill in the entire country.

What is left after a ship has been broken is too small to be counted unless you count lives. The residue occurs in two forms—liquid and powder. The liquid will always be several hundred gallons of diesel fuel, refinery oil, insecticide, complex polymers, dyes, and fishery waste. It's the sludge you see along the coast. The powders will be invisible, occurring only as a haze hanging over the yard: it's made up of asbestos, silicon, steel filings, wood ash, and PCBs. Mixed together they form a gray paste or a gray-white dust that reminds you of Seattle mornings. When it settles on the water, it shines like a mirror for days, killing all marine life for one to two miles out to sea. The workers clean the shore by shoveling contaminated sand into levees and connecting them into one long road that parallels every shipbreaking operation in the world and separates the shore from the shantytown. Such roads can run for miles at six or eight feet above the gradient. Some of them require tunnels to cross from one side to the other. I once drove the shore road at Alang, drunk, late at night when it was most spectacular, speeding from one end to the other, just to watch the places where the sand was on fire, like the road into hell.

But the road at Gbambhala is no more than eight inches above grade. It gives an unobstructed view of the beach. On our left is the town, separated from us by a flooded ditch with numerous plank bridges. A mob of children chases our jeep past hanging clothes, cook fires, and the tangle of ropes that seem to hold the encampment together. Sammy looks like an adult as he drives, sounding the horn with an air of grave responsibility and waving casually at the youngsters who chase us like tattered ghosts. On the right are the ships, twenty medium-sized cargo vessels already grounded and another sixty trawlers and smaller craft being picked apart. Among the sharp-angled shadows of late afternoon we can see figures swarming over each corpse like an army of ants. That's the first thing that comes to mind; but they do not look like beached whales, these ships. They look like toppled buildings. Or like train wrecks at the edge of the ocean. And at first you cannot grasp what has happened because it does not seem logical that human beings would deliberately create this kind of destruction.

Sammy tells me that Robert N'mburo is supervising the lifting of the propeller shaft from the engine room of one of the freighters. We drive to the high tide line and begin to walk the rest of the way. They've made a path of palm fronds in honor of my visit. Everything has been arranged.

Farther out to sea are the silhouettes of another hundred vessels, all waiting for a vacant slot on the beach, some anchored, one already building up cruising speed. We stop and listen to the radioman fifty yards below us. He's directing the captain and engineer on a tanker that seems to be headed away from shore. "*Sendai Maru*, what is your heading?"

A barely recognizable English squawk comes back to him, "Heading two nine zero."

"Very well. Your distance from the port ship?"

"Eight cables. Closing to seven cables. Seven point oh."

"Very well, *Sendai*. Come to course zero-four-zero. Ahead one half."

"Zero-four-zero. Ahead one half."

The radioman drives a blinking red beacon into the sand as the huge ship begins its turn and gathers speed. Someone calls off course changes in degrees. A few men in *lungis* and turbans wander down to our section of beach to watch. After ten minutes the radioman gives a new set of instructions. "*Sendai*, come to one-one-zero. Ahead two-thirds. Please confirm, you are ballasting, yes?"

"Course one-one-zero. Ahead two-thirds. We are continuing to ballast, and we have your light."

"Very well, call out your course."

The ship seems to grow shorter as its bow swings to face us; then, for a long time, it seems not to be moving at all. There is another exchange of numbers over the radio and an acknowledgment from the captain that he is giving full power. The ship itself appears to be no closer to shore than it was twenty minutes before, though its shape has changed to a dark and bulging V atop a churning foam. Soon the bow wake resembles a cat's paw flicking at the water ahead. Then it becomes more of a sound pushing the men back from the wavelets. They plod upslope in twos and threes, as if to prove that they do not yet need to run. The rushing torrent of my imagination gradually becomes a jetlike roar competing with the engine's deep thum-thum-thum, both sounds merging at last into a concussion that seems to have swept in from some World War II battlefield, a sound that is not so much sound as it is a physical pressure in the lungs, a rhythm in the stomach. It is the moment that language becomes useless. As the V expands into a mountainous slope of metal, the wake itself reaches us first as a fine mist that we inhale and then wipe from our faces. When the keel strikes bottom, there is not the shriek that I expect but rather a totally unexpected slippage to one side as if the *Sendai Maru* had suddenly decided to avoid an unpleasant puddle. As the stern fishtails, the bow continues its slow progress, another indication of the vast power that has been put in play.

Some of the sand spills to either side like a huge furrow being cut into the face of the earth, but most of it simply disappears under the broadening shadow of the hull, now rising impossibly high above us. A shallow depression forms for thirty yards on both sides of the prow, which the tide and the ship's own bilges immediately fill. It is as though a giant has suddenly stepped away from the shore and nature now rushes to seal the vacuum. Long after the propeller loses its purchase, the *Sendai Maru* continues her course inland, her plates groaning under an earthly weight that they were never designed to bear and revealing a crusty underside that no one is meant to see.

I have heard that, from time to time, a man will break away from the crowd and rush down the shore as one of these ships emerges from the water under full power and is no longer controllable by the hand of any pilot. Whether from an excess of bravado or out of a desire to commit suicide, it is impossible to say. He stares out to sea as if indifferent to the danger or hypnotized by the prospect of something better and far away. Then, when the ship makes that final sideways lurch, he is either spared by blind chance or else simply annihilated, ground into the sand by abrasions above and below. In either case, he is rarely seen again.

I know of course that the *Sendai Maru* has never been animated by anything other than her engines, but in the sudden silence I am struck by the paradox that something has indeed just died. For a moment no one moves. It's like the awkward hush at graveside after the last prayer and the benediction. And I know that in the morning's low tide tiny creatures will swarm over this ship and begin to dismantle the body. But for one shared moment we keep quiet, each one of us with his private thoughts. Even I, counting what has been lost.

It is one of the sad and fundamental principles of maritime law that a ship out of water is no longer a ship, but a heap of metal. Like a marriage out of love.

Sammy steers me toward another ship farther down the beach.

We reach Robert N'mburo's wreck by walking over a plank pathway thrown across deep ruts in the sand and then after a few moments by wading to a rough scaffolding. Sammy takes off his sandals and throws them on the beach. I roll my trousers and tie my shoes to the briefcase because I remember reading that most deaths in the shipbreaking industry actually occur from tetanus and bacterial infections that began in simple cuts. I will return to my shoes as soon as I reach deck and then will watch my step thereafter. From that one thought arises a mild concern that grows, as we ascend the scaffolding, into a unreasoning fear that literally no one in the world knows where I am. I could slip and fall into the sea at any moment; I could be electrocuted by any one of the land lines snaking from arc lamps on deck down into the water and across the beach to a sputtering generator; or I could step onto a metal gangway that collapses like a fire escape tearing loose from rotting bricks and mortar. No one would know, because I've lied to Narissa and put myself into the hands of a child named Sammy. I could die like one of the workers. And for the first time I realize that I could be replaced just as easily.

I go over the railing and onto the deck with slow and careful movements, clutching the briefcase as if it were an infant.

Below us a man climbs the anchor chain with no more effort than someone climbing a flight of stairs. He disappears into the hawsehole, and after a moment comes the crackle of an acetylene torch and the haunting glow of blue-white light, as if he had been a ghost opening the door of another world. Already the ship has been relieved of her wood, glass, plastic, rubber, porcelain, canvas, hemp, copper, brass, and silver. What is left is a world of iron and a world of iron sounds. We have to shout now to hear each other because most of the "cutting" at this stage is done with sledgehammers. Acetylene torches are rare and precious in this part of the world, and they are dangerous, slicing into pockets of every vaporized chemical that can be hauled by ship and not infrequently exploding. This ship, like most, is simply being beaten apart and hauled away by hand, a process that takes up to a year for the supertankers that are the prized treasure-ships of men like Robert N'mburo, and the principal killers of his men. As we stand on the half-deck and peer into the canyon beneath us, it is like looking into a village that had been bombed from the air.

We step through a maze of cables and descend the first stair to a point perhaps twelve feet below the scuppers, a place that's shadowed by the uppermost hull plates and where we pause to adjust our eyes like men stepping into a darkened theater. In this dim twilight we have to be careful to step over buckets of bolts, coiled electrical wires, and one-inch steel plates stacked like rusty playing cards. Below us are more landings and more metal stairs, all taking odd turns and occasionally hanging like catwalks where former walls have been stripped away. The infrequent shafts of light coming from portholes resemble spotlights focused on the backstage machinery of an experimental drama, and I feel like an actor descending to some unseen production by M. C. Escher. The hammering, which should have echoed like gunshots, becomes no more than a faint tinkling, perhaps muffled by the insane geometry of the demolition or perhaps simply swallowed by the immensity of the ship. It is like walking into a skyscraper that someone has left lying on its side. I go with one hand on a railing and one, where possible, flat against the inner hull. Down and down, past cabins and storage holds, at each level getting a glimpse of the ant-men at work, some banging with sledges, some hauling out miles of intestines, some carrying away iron slabs like leaf-cutters deep in the Amazon.

At last we reach a narrow passage leading through two iron hatches to the orlop, a half-deck just above the bilges where waste spills into the open ocean twenty feet below. The entire stern of our ship has already been cut away, and the unguarded view of the outer harbor, in less dangerous circumstances, might have looked like early evening from one of the antiseptic balconies of a cruise ship. There are the murmuring breakers below us, the quaint commercial vessels at a distance, and a reddening sun that must be setting Brazil ablaze. High above the artificial horizon is our evening star, a sparkling hole in the hull where a torch has just cut through. The sparks fall for thirty feet and then skid down the inner hull like marbles of molten glass.

Someone behind us says, "It looks like an amphitheater, doesn't it?"

The unexpected accent startles me more than actual violence would have done, and the man's demeanor seems almost as alien as my own.

Taller than Sammy, and far more substantial in body, he resembles in my imagination a professional athlete or an American diplomat who has dressed in the local costume for an afternoon of celebrity touring.

"Whenever I look up from this point," he continues, "I always think of one of those paintings of nineteenth-century surgeries, you know, the ones with the medical students peering down into the pit, the one light playing off the surgeon in his bloody apron and cravat—and of course the very pale lady on the table." He chuckles at some private amusement and extends a hand.

"Charles Allemand," I say. "You must be Mr. N'mburo."

"Yeah. For about a year now. Before that I was a white guy like you." The man I had come four thousand miles to meet waits to see if I will laugh. He studies me with an intensity that would have been considered rude, even insulting, in most African cultures. "You look a little wet," he says. "Why don't you chuck that overboard," he nods at my briefcase, "and let's sit and talk for a while. I've got a feeling you're going to miss your flight."

His words are both casual and sinister, like those of a soldier who's grown indifferent to death and to high-sounding causes. When he comes closer, I see that fate has in fact touched him. There is a bandage hanging loose at one palm like a boxer's hand wrapping. A gray scar over his left eye. And as he walks it becomes apparent that he favors one leg and that he is gradually being bent under whatever weight he has chosen to bear. Still, there's nothing wounded about his voice, and he speaks like a man who expects his words to have an effect. He lowers himself to his haunches and rests his elbows on his knees the way I had seen the Bassa people doing in pictures.

I say to him, "Maybe you'll forgive me for suggesting that you're not exactly what I expected."

"No shit?"

"You're American?"

"Used to be. Used to be a lot more than that."

"I see."

"I doubt that, chief. I doubt you have any idea what you're seeing."

"Look, Mr. N'mburo, or Mr. . . ."

"Rosello. Can you believe that? Somewhere along the line my family must have been owned by the only slaveholders in Brooklyn. You think that might have been it? Now, I myself find the name Robert Rosello far stranger than anything I'm about to tell you."

"I appreciate that. But I want you to understand that I'm not here to do anything other than . . ."

"I know why you're here. I even have an idea of how much you're getting paid to cradle your little briefcase. I could tell old Sammy there, but he wouldn't believe that there's that much money in the world. This is a strange place, Chuck. A very strange place indeed. I want you to think about that. Then toss your goodies out into the surf there. And then listen carefully."

"I'm afraid I can't do that."

"Let me ask you something. Have things been going well for you since you got here?"

"How do you mean?"

"Me, I had a headache for weeks. Sinus, diarrhea, heat exhaustion. It takes a while to adapt, let me tell you. Then, after you adapt, it's a pretty good sign that you're going to end up like everybody else around here. Seen anything yet that makes you want to stay?"

"If I could just get you to sign these papers . . ."

"Chuck, listen to me. I'm the guy they sent out here before you."

"I'm sorry, I don't . . ."

"Listen to what I'm saying. I want you to toss the papers. Tell them nobody's signing anything. Tell them the breaking yard is staying open."

"For God's sake why? This place is a disaster. It's killing every man who works here and the environment too."

"You're right. And, besides that, you own it—or at least your clients own it. And they can shut it down, make a few bucks by selling off the scrap, and win the corporate clean-up award all in one afternoon. Is that still the plan?"

"It doesn't make any difference whether you sign or not. If you're the guy they sent out here before me, then you already know that."

"It can delay things, and that's all we want."

"It won't make any difference in the end."

"Nothing makes any difference in the end, Chuck. It's the middle that counts. And, whatever else happens, it's better than starving to death. Right? Every man out there understands that, except here's what he understands that you don't understand. When he starves, his family starves, and not just his immediate family either. Ever watch anybody starve to death? It's like cancer without the tumors. But for every man who dies in the breaking yard there are ten trying to take his place. Why? Because where they come from it's worse."

"You're preaching."

"Damn right I am."

"You're preaching to the wrong person."

"No, I'm preaching to the right person. You're a scumbag, Charles. I want you to do what scumbags always do."

"Which is?"

"Look out for yourself. Switch sides. I want you to drop a monkey wrench into the corporate makeover. I want you to lose your luggage. Whatever would cause a delay, that's what I want you to do."

"Wouldn't that be a slight conflict of interest?"

"Not if you came over to our side."

"Simple as that, eh?"

"Simple as that."

"And what I would gain for myself out of all this would be precisely what?"

"If we can get a long enough delay, we can form a corporation under Liberian law, a genuine co-op where the workers would own principal interest. Then we could begin modernizing, cleaning up, and paying a guy like you."

"Sorry."

"It could work."

"Maybe in the Land of Oz. Not here. You've got real problems out there, Robert. And I've got a plane to catch. So maybe next time. We'll do the whole world peace thing together. Nice meeting you. But don't get up; I can show myself out."

"That's what we thought you'd say."

I feel a sudden chill. A door bangs shut. And it occurs to me once again that no one knows where I am. I look up from the pit of his amphitheater and see faces looking back. My head aches, and I understand that if I sit down with this man I will be negotiating for my life.

I stand very still, looking at Robert N'mburo for a long time, trying to imagine him organizing documents at a conference table. I try to imagine him in the finest suits and sitting in leather chairs. Summoning his morning coffee with the push of a button, like me. It is a leap my mind cannot make. Robert is too scarred and warped, too taken by the life he's chosen, and probably, I realize, quite simply insane from the suffering he has seen. So I take a slow breath and consider my options. I do not sit. I do not make sudden motions. I do not look down at the churning sea.

I negotiate.

We begin with little things, the warp and woof of life among the lowly. I promise him oranges, dates, and cheese. Soy milk and wheat. Torches and winches and trucks. Within minutes we are outside of all reality, my own words sounding as hollow as those of any politician. Only the gathering darkness suggests that there can be any end to this babbling, to my judicious monotone. And although the man across from me seems mesmerized, I do not doubt the truth—that he's following these words the way a cobra follows the flute.

I promise him medicine, tools, and fuel. Then books and building materials. Fresh water. Maybe a school. Whatever, in a word, might sound reasonable to a man who has lost his reason. But it is not enough. His darkened face grows darker, and I see the sadness that precedes some violent act. When he starts to stand, I know we've reached the end. I've tried and found no argument-stopping words. Now it's the shuffling mob or the foam beneath the stern.

And one last chance. Robert looks at my briefcase, raises his eyebrows in silent question, and seems unsurprised that I find the courage to shake my head. But it's all I've got. We both know the gesture won't help. And he starts to walk away.

From some deep well I hear a voice, quite clearly, proclaim, "Give me Sammy then."

It stops him and turns his head.

And suddenly I'm saying, "There's a midnight plane to Marrakech. Passports if you have the dollars. And if I can get him into France . . ."

He looks at Sammy and then looks at me, the muscles knotting at his jaw.

"I can do it. You know I can."

"Not just to France. All the way to America?" He's bargaining again. I can hear the hope in his voice and something else, a hint of something else in my own.

"All the way."

"You swear?"

"On the life of my son."

"And until he's grown?"

"Yes."

"You swear this?"

"Robert—listen to me. I can save him. You know I can."

River Story

FOR SUSAN

Behavioral and personality changes are often the first signs of CNS
involvement. Later more florid psychological changes may occur, with
hallucinations or delusions. Reversion of sleep rhythm is characteristic,
with drowsiness during the day, a feature from which the disease derives
its name. Other nervous symptoms include tremor, most characteristically
of the face and lips, and hyperesthesia, causing some patients to avoid
common practices such as closing or locking doors. Without treatment,
the patient's level of consciousness progressively deteriorates.
      —Quinn, *African Trypanosomiasis*

I have the sleeping sickness. I believe that Brawley has it too, so I watch
him very carefully.

   I watch him focus on the flies, reaching rather than swatting with
the hand that holds his cigarette. Half a swarm buzzes up through the
smoke, settling on the lip of his glass, strutting like soldiers on parade,
and he begins to quarrel without even looking in my direction. "Okay,
here's the problem," he tells me. "World's got no lost cities anymore,
right? Blokes like you and me? This is it. I mean what I'm sayin', Jocko.
This—right here—is it. *That's* the problem." And pecks at the table
with blunt fingers, scattering ashes without disturbing the insect world
around him. "Jesus Christ, I'm sweatin'. What time is it?"

"Eight o'clock."

"I'm sweatin' like the dengue 'n it ain't even eight o'clock yet. And lookit that fog. Out there on the river an' all. You know wha' that means? Means today's gonna be stinking bloody hell and a half, that's what." While we watch the barge drift closer, waiting for the inevitable collision and the sharp, satisfying sounds of disaster.

I let the flies drink from the back of my hand. They are not tsetse flies; they're handsome iridescent creatures, quick, alert, top-of-the-line flies, as green and glowing as peacock feathers. The tsetse is drab and slow, a gray-brown unattractive fly that drinks from below the skin. It owns this part of Africa. That's what I've learned.

Brawley tries to smoke himself into consciousness, studying the grain of the tabletop, listening suspiciously to beggars and fruit vendors below us. Their bellow and cry. After a while he shifts his squint to a European couple besieged at one end of the market—something about them that he doesn't like. "You know they got French tourists in Machu Picchu? You know that? Amer'can teenagers all over Kathmandu and no place to get lost at. You hear what I'm sayin'? I seen whole Jap families up there at Abu Simbel crawling across the feet of Ramses the bloody Second, that's what. Flittin' and crawling about. It's like Edgar Rice Burroughs is dead in this part of the world, how you like that for a report on your life?"

"Nobody knows what you're talking about," I say.

"Oh right. It's you, the Reverend Pogue as I live an' breave. For a minute I thought I was talkin' to Tarzan out here in the eight o'clock my-asma. Luxuriatin' upon this lovely teakwood portico all cantilevered over the edge of hell drinkin' French beer and waiting for them poor bastards out there in the mist to drown. That's what I thought it was. My mistake."

"I buy and sell unclaimed freight," I say. "That's all."

"Right."

The barge comes to rest about noon, impaling itself on half-rotten pilings near the inlet while the passengers cheer and sing, a rich chaos of joy and relief. It all happens so slowly that they think they were safe. Kingfishers and spoonbills continue their feeding along the shore; even the tiny, nervous flycatchers in the overhanging branches give no more than a momentary flutter. No one in the market cries out. We simply stare. Even Verloc, the café owner, limps onto the portico carrying a pair of binoculars, counting his profit perhaps. Who can blame him? They are caught in the current, and we watch like dog-faced baboons while they gather at the rail and give the barge a heavy list, the three of us thinking they don't even know, they don't have any idea. Because at the first brittle crackling, at the slow shriek of wood upon metal, they cheer. And we watch. There is nothing you can do.

This is how they return from upriver sometimes, the pusher tugs as well as the barges. They do it without fuel or pumps or electric lights, steering for sandy shoals or the safety of mudflats or fragile pilings around some village where diesel fuel gets trucked in twice a month and then gets sold by the quart. Sometimes they drift farther down the main channel to Kinshasa or to us over here in Brazzaville, arriving like floats from some pathetic Mardi Gras, insanely populated, maybe four or five roped together, one leaky hulk after another sagging under secret cargoes and wild stories of Tutsi massacres inland, tributaries choked with bodies that nobody wants to hear about anymore. They stink of fish meal and manioc. They carry hollow-eyed women along the rail, and amputees, and stacks of zebra hides as stiff as cardboard. And live monkeys strung together like convicts. Parrots. Stork-thin children. Diseased chickens. They bring all the groaning, moldering rubbish of the river plus a drunken crewman or two. Except sometimes. Sometimes they bring enough opium or uncut diamonds in someone's belly to make the whole rudderless voyage seem sane.

So I study Verloc's face while he refocuses the binoculars. His only movement is a slight twitch about the mouth when the linesman saves them, a stick figure who goes leaping and tying off before the current can catch the stern and send it spiraling into dark water. I want to applaud, but Verloc and Brawley remain silent, suspicious. Perhaps it's the disease. We wait until the barge is secure, then Verloc sighs slightly and makes his voice as wispy as the fog. "Clever fellows, de Bantu. Like monkeys when dey need to be."

But then someone is already mentioning the others, the abandoned ones, dark unopened metal boxes upon the water, and then immediately after that innocent remark Brawley is cursing, allowing the last of his energy to the proposition that someone is out of his mind.

"We need the money," I simply say.

"They're capsized, you fool, rockin' in the water like corpses. An' even if they got pockets of air, who would want to crawl inside a coffin? Jesus Christ! Tiniest thing'll send 'em into the mud like crab baskets. 'Cept you'd be inside, wouldn't you, drowning for a handful a beads."

"Or diamonds."

"Or nothing at all."

"I'm just saying that, technically, they belong to us."

"They belong to the river now."

"Listen to me. You're not drunk, you're infected. If you're not treated, you're going to die, same as me. That's all I'm saying. I'm just thinking about what it would take to have a future."

"I'm not infected. I'm sick of living li' a pig, that's all."

While they cheer. It's what they all do when they reach Brazzaville; they dance and cheer. It's their right. For some it is the first expression of hope in their lives. So why should we lie awake at night? Even horror has its limits. Something you would think God could learn.

Just before the first showers, a company of men draws the barge close to shore and shoves a plank out from the elephant grass while two freshwater crocs slather down the mudbank below us and drift out to investigate, low in the water, like ironclads from the last century. Then someone is helping Phoolan down the plank. Some ridiculous crewman who does it in the European fashion, with a slight bow as she sets foot on land. The most beautiful woman we have ever seen.

Brawley is picking a bit of tobacco off his tongue, snorting, "Over there, lad."

But I've already seen her.

"That one's lookin' for God, she is. Time to get offyer arse."

Though of course I cannot stir. It's midday, and this is the well of lost souls.

She moves like music through the tumbling chaos, one hand holding a silk *llasa* over her head and shoulders, the other hand flickering among throngs of children, touching their faces, creating smiles. And they seem to know her. Even the beggars strain grotesquely for a passing touch, and her name precedes her up the hill until she reaches the constable's stand and speaks to Old N'Reara in broken French. Something about a man, a lost husband, maybe a father, it's impossible to tell. And then for one moment, when she turns bright gleaming eyes upon me, I grow young.

Later, after Verloc opens the café, I can see the humor of it all. The Americans are here in their canvas vests and straw hats that wilt in the heat. They think the sickness was wiped out along with yellow fever and smallpox, but the joke's on them. And there are European women who take pictures from odd angles, struggling to get bougainvillea into every shot, their long legs glistening, breasts and buttocks shaped by sweat and all the time thinking, dear God, that they are in jungle. Food for flies. They believe I'm a picturesque drunk, some minor character left behind after the film crew's retired. I try not to disappoint, but I'm losing focus. I have the West African variant of the disease, the kind that lingers in the blood for years while you watch yourself waste away. Hallucinate. Sleep. And that brings, oddly enough, long periods of wakefulness during which you cannot stop chattering. Chattering. There's a drug called Suramin. . . . And she is so beautiful, so remarkably out of place, that someone must be dreaming.

I see bobbing black figures swarm over the barge, taking bit by bit the color and the cargo like a string of ants. I can't be sure; I'm floating where the clear bubbles float, just this side of consciousness. I can see that they are leaving behind a wreck, bilges weeping rust, sheet metal buckling around the pilothouse. I can see that. I think I am talking to someone too. I tell her that the last item is an okapi, one of the slender, short-necked giraffes that live in the upper basin near Kisangani. Gentle animals inhabiting dense forest where their larger cousins can't live. Better get a shot of this; they're extremely rare. No, I say, okapis don't have the spots or the long neck of the plains giraffe. Yes, they look a bit like llamas with short hair and intelligent faces. Most don't survive the trip to Western zoos. This one is a young female who's already sensed the crocodiles gathering beneath the stern; she's stamping and straining in fear, wearing a raw place on her neck where the twin ropes rub. When the men try to lead her away, she goes into a frenzy, kicking and thrashing like a horse, drawing the reptiles half out of the water, jaws levered wide and hissing in anticipation.

Brawley ambles over to us while the fat woman is snapping furiously, and he begins a running monologue over her shoulder. "It's got no animal language, you know, the o-kapi. Lives its whole life in silence like your true giraffe of the savannahs. 'Cept for that kind of barking sound that you hear. Prolly just trying to get its bref. I mean if you had six blokes on you an' a rope around your neck, right?"

"What if it falls over the side?" her husband asks.

"Not bloody likely. Live o-kapi's worth a year's pay to any of them black fellows down there, dead one's not worth beer money."

Finally the barking becomes no more than a hoarse cough, and the animal lets them tie its legs together and wrestle it to the deck. Four of the men hold her while two others try to drive away the crocs with long poles, poking them and provoking a grotesque, churning dance beneath the stern. After a half hour nothing has changed. One of the men goes below deck and returns with a pipe, giving half a dozen two-handed blows to the okapi's head before it slumps. Then they carry their prize to the warehouse with no further trouble and lay her beside the other supplies.

I'm inexplicably angry. My hand shakes. I remember Brawley reaching for the flies and hate him with surprising suddenness as I sink toward sleep. It's early afternoon, and the beautiful safety of sleep. It's coming, I can feel it, the leafy shade like a familiar blanket slowly drawn up to the shoulder and nestled beneath the chin. I can barely hear them now, the fat German tourist in a tirade, Brawley's smooth cynicism; and I would not take the Suramin if a priest offered it as communion. I'm almost there. A slow blink gives me the beautiful woman once more, how she stands out among the jostling bodies below us. Like royalty. They won't even step into her shadow. And I can smell the rain now, thickening, preparing itself while the voice I can't escape whispers, "Lovely face, absolutely lovely. Don't need a sharp eye for that, eh? Wonder what she's brought to market. I mean besides the obvious." And when I awake, she's there on the portico with Verloc, his hazy image snickering and bobbing just like the toothless old men who shield their eyes and lift the open palm.

Brawley's trying to drag me awake, hoarse with the hilarity of his message. "Hey Pogue," he seems to be saying. "Hey Pogue, guess what? She's a thief."

I blink, still lost within a world of green.

The bougainvillea along the south shore of our inlet begins at the water's edge and rises in a tangle so thick that the Sangha people call it monkey puzzle after a tree that grows along their own tributary in northern Zaire. Creepers and mango build canopy upon canopy in bewildering variation until there's no way to distinguish the surge from anchoring earth; it's simply a green swell that hovers over the last few stalls of our pitiful Casbah and threatens the café itself. During my first year in Africa I would sit on Verloc's deck waiting for one of those autumn storms that gives the impression of being lost at sea and imagine myself on a doomed voyage where drowned sailors mysteriously appear from the depths and speak meaningless clues before being washed overboard again. Ghostly strangers uttering nonsense. Once Verloc himself stepped out into the rain babbling incomprehensibly about teak, insisting that it was not an African wood, did not grow within a thousand miles of Congo. So intensely that for weeks afterward I thought he was insane. Brawley had to reassure me that he was merely drunk. So I'm not surprised to wake inside a dream and hear a ghost croaking, ". . . one of us actually, come to make our for-tune I believe."

"What are you saying?" I manage.

"I'm saying it's time to wake up. Grab opportunity by the balls and all that."

"I don't . . ."

"Looks a bit Chinese, don't she? I mean up close and all, not the color of your ordinary bush babies. One thing for certain, she ain't local. That little trick she's got on looks like a sari? You don't see nothing like that south o' Cameroon. Makes you wonder, don't it?"

"She's a thief?"

"Well, she wants summit off one of them wrecked barges you was yamming about. Wants it bad enough to negotiate if you get my drift."

"And she doesn't speak English?"

"Look at that face, Jocko. That look li' an English face to you?"

"So how did she know to come to us?"

"Anybody could've pointed her this direction; we're not a secret enterprise, you know. This is opportunity, Pogue. Some smiles before she slips away. Besides, what was you saying about needin' a housekeeper now, one that can get by in French, eh?"

"What exactly does she want?"

"Look. All I know's she spent an hour at the pink hotel. Where the diamond merchants are, right? And then the gods, the gods, Pogue, set 'er down here at which point you start playin' detective. That don't go in this part of the world."

"What's her name?"

He turns to Phoolan for the first time and addresses her in halting French. "You got to forgive the reverend, miss, he's been a bit paralyzed since his big discovery. But no need to worry; we got all the records *and* the salvage rights. You come to the proper place."

She does not seem confused or frightened.

"We deal with all the big companies, we do. Import, export, whatever. My partner here has just temporarily lost his capacity for astonishment. He's actually very glad to make your acquaintance."

She sits in the rattan chair and studies me, rather like a queen. Her face is unwrinkled, the dark brown of the river itself but not the ebony of inner Africa. Her eyes are neither kind nor cruel but simply ancient, while the lips seem unnaturally thin and serious. She wears her hair like the Arab women of the north, long and straight, almost like another garment. When she moves, her bracelets make a tiny musical response. And she says to me, "Very well, I will stay."

Brawley breaks in before I can speak. "Of course there'll be a slight fee. You know, for the recovery itself and the tax we got to pay to, ah, local authorities."

When she does not flinch, does not take her eyes from me, we know that it's diamonds.

It's early morning, and I am alive. I see shadows as sharp as zebra stripes and hear the drone of a single fly. The fog will be rising soon, but for the moment there are no ambiguities, and I know that there is someone in my house. I smell her. It's such a welcome certainty that I simply walk toward the *ktala*, where we cook and eat during the rainy season, and she is there. Like magic. But I am not sleepwalking. I am not dreaming. She is there, and I am acutely aware of her face, the familiar beauty of it and also the mystery. I see her rocking over a wooden board, kneading in the Western manner, pushing the dough with the heel of her hand and turning the mass into itself, keeping her arms straight and rolling the wrists so that the bracelets chime delicately and her breasts are shaped into loaves.

Who is she?

I try to remember and see a kaleidoscope of changing shapes.

It is such a clever disease, forever changing its mind. At times I hear colors and see sounds that no sane man can imagine. At other times I simply sleep. Some days I babble to invisible beings, and some days they babble back. It's no fool for consistency. And today I am here, alone, in the moment. Have no memory at all.

There is a woman in my house. I see her. I feel her every movement from across the room, the warm dough yielding to her hands. It is impossible, I know, but I hear her hair rustling against itself and the soft exhalation at her lips. She is there. So intensely there that the walls give way and blur.

Is she my wife?

What is her name? I open my mouth, but it's no use.

I try twice again. There's nothing there, until finally I realize that I don't need a name because the air is heavy with bread, as moist and inviting as earth's womb, and that I'm a willing prisoner. I am happy. This is the opposite of what I fear. She is real, but my memory of her is lost in the past. I'm standing in the present, listing the things I know, counting them off in my mind, one through four, until I have to shrug and smile. Because there is a woman in my house, so beautiful that she creates the world around us.

Her voice, I think, is a voice I've known all my life. She says, "Why does he call you that?" Without prelude, without looking in my direction, the way a wife should say it. "Why does he call you a priest?" In English.

And something possesses me. I feel words forming, tumbling out in perfect order, and I am not dreaming, not remembering. I'm being born. I say, "It's his little game."

"A game?" she says. "It is his little game?"

"I'm not a priest, but a long time ago, when I came here, I was a missionary. A Mormon missionary."

"Roland Pogue." As if the two names don't fit together. "You are no longer missionary?"

"No."

"But American?"

"I don't know."

"Both of you are *nagana*—sleepers?"

Now I'm chuckling, like a drunk trying to untwist his tongue. "I'm not anything at the moment. I buy and sell unclaimed freight. Is that what you want to know?"

"You are making a joke?"

"Yeah. I'm making a joke."

"A Moslem cannot do such a thing. It is forbidden."

"Not Moslem, Mormon."

She considers but does not reply for a time. Finally, she says, "You steal from the dead?"

"No, His Excellency Chundai Boraka, second cousin of the Interior Minister, steals from the dead. We just get a cut for keeping the books straight and tidying up a bit."

"You are a joking man, Roland Pogue."

"Not really. Let me tell you something: a human being will do any damn thing in the world for a nickel. I know. It's what I've come to believe. Anything to survive. And that includes me and you."

"You mock us. You mock the gods."

Without knowing her name I know what will happen. I realize now. I feel peace. I feel a tranquility that I've not felt for years, as deep and comforting as sleep. Because I remember what is happening. That soon she will turn and take me into her arms, drawing every fiber of my being into her. Like the first man who fell on his knees before the first woman and pressed his face against her and knew it was a taste of the eternal.

"Who are you?" I whisper.

And not yet turning, she tells me, "I am the goddess Phoolan."

It is a strange disease. There are times when I am content to call it reality and times when I think I will go mad without the treatment. It comes and goes. I see things. I hear voices. I doubt the world, and the world doubts me. But at this instant I am certain of one thing, that she is in my house. And one thing more. That I am awake. And yet one more. That this eternal moment is all I need. "I'm not sure I understand."

"I don't require your understanding," she says. Kneading the dough, rolling her wrists the way they do, and lifting her breasts to me.

"I don't think she trusts me," says Brawley.

It's afternoon. I'm saying to him, "What makes you think that?"

And he is telling me, "Because she wants you to go into the hull. Alone."

"When did she tell you that?"

"Yesterday. While you was spreadin' goodwill among the less fortunate of the earth."

"What exactly did she say?"

"She said she knew which barge it was 'cause o' the numbers on the side. That most of it was above wa'er and she'd tell you when the time was right."

"She'd tell *me*?"

"Right."

"I'd be going in alone?"

"Lissen to me. Lissen! You can go crazy when this's over, right? You can go to sleep. You can go native. You can go to hell or Hi-waiee, don't nobody care. But I seen this much with my own eyes—are you lissenin' to me!—I seen 'em smuggle out diamonds big as your fucking 'ead. Right? Now the question is wha' are we gonna do—ask one of your pi'aninny friends to go in for you?"

"I was delivering medical supplies. Yesterday I mean. I was delivering medical supplies out at one of the squatter camps."

"Don't you go babbling off on me, Pogue, I'll smack you three days from tomorra."

"I went back to the mission for a while. I took them some supplies. That's all."

"Fine. I'm not worried about yesterday or the day before that. An' I don't mind your porkin' the missus or followin' her around like she was the Queen of the Nile, but this 'ere is business. And good enough business means we get out o' this hellhole forever. Make a clear start."

"I'm not going inside one of those barges."

"Yesterday you was interested. Three days ago you'd dive into a sewer for a dime. Now you got scruples."

"Forget it."

"Lissen to me, Pogue. She's a thief. In this part o' the world a thief is a profession, not a crime. Survival. That's wha' we talkin' about, innit? Survival."

"I said no."

"All right, but think about this. How come she picks you, eh? Cause you're the only whiteface bloke around? Cause o' your debonair charm? Your vast powers of men'al concentration? Why you? Answer me that."

"Why don't you shut up."

"Oh, that's a clever one. Can't nobody get the best of you, can we now?"

"Shut up."

Brawley drops his head into his hands. For a long time he says nothing, and I let the breeze take me away. I'm drifting out over the river where it's morning again and the fog rises to meet me, where I can inhale and look gigantically down upon the ruins of conquest. I think of Conrad. Hemingway. I think of Louis Leakey in a dry gorge, brushing away a continent with his brushes. And of her.

From far away I can hear him saying, "They got a shipment. Over there in Kinshasa. Shipment from the States, couple of cases of that Surymin. N'Reara's brother-in-law or somethin'. Says there's a doctor'll get you a course o' treatment for a thousand dollars American. Might be just a rumor, might be true."

"Why are you telling me?"

"'Cause. Blokes like you and me. Nothing else out there, Pogue. Nothing. Blue Nile's already been discovered. Victoria Falls. Killy-monjare-o. Zimbabwe. No diamond nuggets just lying there on the riverbank—not here, not anywhere else in Africa. You understand what I'm sayin', Pogue?"

"I hear you."

"No more Stanley and Livingstone. No more pyramids. No lost city of gold. This is it. This is all we get. No more safari. This, right here, is it. And I hate this fuckin' hellhole. I don't know how I got here in the first place. But I need another river, Pogue. A clean one."

I remove my socks for no good reason and drape them delicately over a stanchion, trying, I suppose, to delay the instant when I open the hatch and inhale the darkness. So I think of socks. How disposable they are, how unnecessary in most of the world. How frightened I am of cutting my feet when I descend. So now I sit on the side of the pilot-house and lace my shoes tightly, making mechanical effort. Working with unnecessary precision, the way old fishermen mend their nets. And I am a painted man, coated with muck from half-wading, half-crawling across the mudflat, greased on the outside and unrecognizable even to myself. The air is damp, so I move comfortably without cracking or creaking.

The barge rests on its side in about eight feet of water, the stern fully submerged and the numbers 687 cut diagonally by the waterline. It's singing to me. Creaking metal upon metal above me, a lower moaning from below. Wavelets nudging a log rhythmically against the deck. A trickle, a scratching from the stern. I catch myself thinking too much about the canted world beneath me, the microcosmic darkness, and so reach for the hatch. It swings open with surprising ease.

Vague light extends two or three feet along an iron ladder that's been twisted into tendrils. I test it before giving it my full weight and then descend, more outward than down. Take my first breath of tainted air. It is a sweet smell, not the horrifying stench of earthly decay nor the putrefaction of fish. It's sweet, like molasses, and I decide to do without the handkerchief, pulling myself several more rungs into the hold and trying to judge the distance to the opaque glistening surface below. Then take a second breath and a third. Pause to tell myself that this is not a tomb. And wonder if it is only my imagination that the interior water level seems so far beneath the surface of the river. I try tapping the bulkhead with my knuckles, but it tells me nothing.

While my eyes adjust to the gloom, I try to orient myself to a world thrown askew. The barge's port side will be the deck when I drop; the keel will be starboard; the man I am after will have been washed to the stern with other loose cargo. With a bit of luck I can be out in five minutes. Why do I hesitate? I hear flycatchers outside, the faraway grunting of crocodiles, even some human speech wafting across the water. Inside there is only a tiny trickle of bubbles coming from the submerged engine compartment. So why do I hesitate?

I ease myself over the handrail, hold my breath, and drop. It's only a foot and a half before I hit metal, but the shock is multiplied by a thunderous doom and the subtle slant of the floor. The sharp pain comes first, a burning that tells me one ankle has been sliced by something I can't see. I go sprawling, sliding into oily water, taking in great gulps as I struggle for air and stability. I'm afraid I'll take hold of the sharp thing, but my arms are working automatically, my hands grasping for anything, legs pumping. I'm like a man trying to climb a slippery bank, not able to swim, not able to stand, only floundering ridiculously while his energy gives out. Finally I fall back shivering with the realization that I've swallowed a quantity of what I'm lying in. Water that is no longer water.

I think to myself I'm going to die for a pouch full of diamonds, and who says that God does not have a sense of humor? With that calm realization, I find that I can stand, the water being no more than ten inches deep. It moves. I've given life to dozens of floating objects: a carpenter's saw with its black blade just under the surface, a wooden crate, two ebony masks, bits of plastic, a red and white gasoline drum, a child's toy boat perfectly upright and undamaged. And much nearer, almost at my feet, a gray, wrinkled hand. It's a peculiar, dizzying view that I take in, like looking down from a cloud. Things are crooked, canted, static, fluid. There's no horror now; I see a world with its own beauty—a soft coating of silt on the inner hull, a chemical sheen rising and falling with the ripples. I wade farther back into the darkness with no fear, looking for the man she described.

There's no need to search. The barge is as suddenly familiar as my own house. They are clustered near the stern hatch and frozen in grotesque postures. Two of them clutched in each other's arms like lovers, curious, twisted expressions on their faces. The next one lying with his face in the water, head bobbing quaintly because of the wavelets I've made. The others are tumbled together in an indistinguishable mass, their faces also gray and bloated. Nine of them in all. I wade toward them, sorting by size and shape, recalling the clues she'd given me: the armband, the shell necklace, the shoulder tattoo. In the end, though, he is the one who finds me. Something soft that caresses my calf, inviting me to stay a moment longer.

I do not jerk away but rather stoop to his level, contemplating his rest, raising the arm enough to see that scavengers have begun their work without human protest or hollow emotion. He's simply sleeping, and I work my way back along the body until I come to the ankle. There, just as she has said, is a leather pouch.

Now I am outside, again contemplating my socks, cupping a leather pouch, its irregular shape the only evidence I need of my visit. I am sitting next to my crusted socks, dry, stiff shapes next to the pilothouse, dark liquid draining away from me in rivulets. A metallic taste in my mouth. The distance and detachment of the descent are leaving me, and now my hands are shaking as I draw open the bag. I hold it close to my stomach so they will not spill over the deck, and pour. Finally I understand.

There is one shape only, and I rotate it in my hand, tiny droplets of water sparkling in the late morning sun. Beautiful, exquisite in workmanship, the variations in wood perfectly matching its true colors in the wild. It is a small fetish, one of the handsomely carved figurines from the central highlands, fine grained and alive, though strangely silent. An okapi.

We never saw her again. Brawley searched throughout the Old Quarter for days, then in the market and in the hotels along the Boulevard de 30 Juin. In the Cité. The shantytown. Everywhere there'd been glimpses and rumors. A beggar told me that he had seen her giving out coins, a beautiful, fair-skinned woman with green eyes from the north. And some of the children swore they'd got food from her while she'd been wrapped in rags and smiles, a fat grandmother with a basket of sweets. A prostitute. The wife of an emir. A spirit-bird. A cool breeze for an old man closing his eyes for the last time. They were certain, all of them.

After several weeks Brawley followed her—upriver—on one of the pusher tugs that promised to go beyond Kisangani. I waved as they went churning toward midchannel, and he waved from the stern. For a long time I watched him through the binoculars, strutting and squawking among the crew, drinking from a brown bottle and bending at the waist, choking, gagging, laughing, triumphantly strangled and hugely satisfied with himself. Like one of the parrots outside of Auguste Verloc's café.

In the Picking Room

1

Okay, here's my baseball fantasy.

I'm somewhere in that dry wasteland between first and second when I look up, and what do I see? On the far horizon I see a silhouette that might be the third base coach on a trampoline, already four feet in the air, knees almost touching his chin, and cranking one arm like a wild man. Which tells me I can make it even though baserunning is not my skill. Because in real life? I am too slow, too heavy, just too damn big for anything. But on this particular night, with the stadium lights like Hollywood, it's going to be different. So I round second, pushing off from that bag like it was the end of the earth. Chugging for third. And about halfway there, I fling myself into the atmosphere, flying like a bulldozer dropped out of a cargo plane because I'm a hell of a big guy, and I get maybe one gulp of free air before I'm plowing into that powdery earth so hard that it cuts a trench under the glove. I mean throwing dirt like a meteorite striking the desert. And I slide, man, I slide until that left toe touches canvas at precisely zero miles an hour. Like a ballerina, Jack. And there he is. Blue is looking down on me like Sweet Jesus, dripping sweat and fanning air with both arms, telling the world I'm as safe as a baby in its crib, yes sir. While the crowd goes wild.

And I know that's not much. But I don't have much. And it's the best I've got on most days because we live in a crumbling world and if I blink just once I'm back in the picking room. Picking cloth. I'll be holding one hand like this, getting ready to whack the dust off my uniform, and then there he'll be, Pardue or maybe Murtaugh, swinging around the end of the aisle, saying, ". . . the hell are you doing now, you moron?" And then I guess the crowd goes pretty quiet.

Because in the real world they don't use binners and pickers anymore. The textile mills are failing, and the jobs are leaving for Pakistan, and there's nothing on the horizon but scaffolding and empty bins. And maybe somebody yelling out over the floor, "Hey, y'all! Riggs is in Las Vegas. Doing his act."

That's what'll make them laugh.

2

On the day they fired Kutschenko I was a binner, slow as an ox but steady enough to know I would last as long as Murtaugh. If the layoffs didn't get me first. It was a simple job. You pushed a dolly of cloth into the picking room, found an aisle with vacant bins, and stacked the rolls—aisle 13, row 6, bin D—the boom echoing every time a roll landed. It was like heaving bodies into the sea. Lift and toss, lift and toss until the paper-shrouded rolls had disappeared into the deep. Then going back for the next load. Eight to ten times an hour. Because the aisles of the picking room were too narrow for a forklift.

So here is the point. One roll of hard-finished denim, papered and spooled, weighs seventy-five pounds. Ten rolls weigh a minute and a half. A hundred rolls weigh a lifetime. So that after six weeks your shoulders and arms were like steel. After a year you were Murtaugh. It's why we earned what we did. They gave us money, and we gave them that hideous strength until we were somebody else. Nobody lasted. Everybody was on the road to somewhere else. A binner is a machine that looks like a man.

So it was like six months before I mentioned it. At lunch, you know, laying back on a stack of boxes, Willie T. and Pardue rolling up their hot dog wrappers and shooting free throws, Murtaugh smoking one after another, and Kutschenko saying, ". . . the hell you doing in that notebook all the time, huh? You look like an ape readin' a matchbook."

"I'm working on material," I said.

"He's working on material," Pardue said.

"What kinna material?"

"What kinna material you working on, kid?"

"Ideas."

"He's working on idea material."

"Will you shut the fuck up. What kinna ideas you working on? Like science ideas or like a novel or something?"

"I don't know, I'm just thinking about giving it a shot, you know, doing a little stand-up. Sometime."

"You mean like comedy?"

"Yeah, like comedy." Which is what got the big laugh.

"Hey, you got a great start already, kid. All people talk about is how your head is bigger than a mule's. Lissen, you gotta have college for that. I mean, you can be funny looking, but that ain't funny, you know what I'm saying? You want to *write* funny, then you got to have the college."

"I don't know. . . ."

"Like whatta you got right now, right there on the page?"

"It's just an idea. It's not really a routine."

"We'll tell you if it's a routine or not."

"Yeah, we'll tell you. Is it a routine, or what?"

"It's just a note," I said. "It's not a routine."

"He's got nothing," said Pardue. "He's working on a science book. I knew it. He's a scientist."

"You don't know," said Willie T. "It could be a routine or something. Let's hear it, boy. Play your note."

"Okay. Okay, here goes. Like, I was just thinking . . . did you ever notice how on television they advertise drugs that you don't even know what they're for?"

"Heartburn," suggested Pardue. "You got your heartburn, and you got your cholesterol."

"Cut it out, give him a chance."

"No, I'm talking about when some announcer says like, 'Ask you doctor about Thorexynol,' and then, bam, your Thorexynol theme music will start up and your Thorexynol theme couple will go walking on the beach and there you are wondering what just got cured. They do that all the time now."

"That's not funny, kid."

"I *know* it's not funny, you dumbass. It's got to be part of a routine, which I already told you I don't have. What you do is work it into a doctor bit, see, like you go to the doctor's office with a broken arm or, you know, impotence or poison ivy or something and ask the doc for some of that Thorexynol because that's what the ad told you to do. Right? When it's really for constipation."

"If it's really for constipation, then what you puttin' it on poison ivy for?"

"How about I kick your ass because you look like a dwarf?"

"I'm just saying. We think you need some new material."

"Hey, kid," said Pardue. "Did you ever notice that you suck? That's what you ought to notice. That funny stuff happens to you all the time and then you tell it and it turns to crapola? Did you ever notice *that*?"

Which is when Meek appeared. Holding the clipboard down below his waist, with the white envelope stuffed in his shirt pocket. Striped tie, short sleeves, beeper clipped to his belt. Everyone knew what it meant. I remembered at that moment nights around our kitchen table with my mother talking about World War II, how the guy from Western Union would bicycle right to your house with his satchel and take out the envelope as he was walking to your door. Everybody knew what that meant too. Except back then we were winning the war.

We knew before he even stepped out of the elevator. All of us looking up when the hoist light came on and the pulley started humming, because no one ever rode the elevator into the picking room. It was a one-way drop, like the caged descent into a coal mine, and you used it twice a day—once going in and once coming out. When the doors finally opened, we saw that it was Meek. The personnel guy. He looked like a child, alone, on a very broad stage, and he waited until the steel doors and the safety gate locked before stepping across the crack. We thought he was a bastard, I suppose, because it never occurred to us that he was simply afraid. When he got to us, he spoke in a low, mournful voice that we all recognized as fake. "Burkhard," he said softly, "could I speak with you? Down in my office?"

"Fuck no," said Kutschenko. "Do it right here. If you're going to do it, you little maggot, you can at least be a man about it. Do it right now."

And that's the funny thing. The paper in the envelope really was pink.

3

The picking room was like a library where the pickers went their dark routes pulling scrolls of cloth from the bins and dropping them into boxes bound for other mills. We sent out boxes by the ton. It's the way they measured us, not by the miles we walked but by the tons we lifted, until the numbers 12/25/E became only the rough coordinates of a seventy-five-pound roll of denim buried under twenty others just like it, headed for China, where it would get its real identity. Then get shipped back to this country as something by Levi, Wrangler, Arizona, Tommy, Ralph, Calvin. Who the hell knew?

It's hard to imagine. A picking room is not like anything else. Not like a warehouse or an aircraft hangar or a cavern. It's just different. I used to tell people to try to imagine a castle or, anyway, something that's old and big like a cathedral, ruined and rebuilt over the years and then one day gutted so that all that remains is a hollow shell and not any kind of building that can be reasoned with. Just an outer wall circling back on itself like some kind of shape a kid would make with building blocks. Then fill that shape with shelves. Miles and miles of them. That's your picking room. So that some sections of the outer wall might look like a ruined temple, like any stiff wind could blow it away particle by particle. Then in other places you might find a master mason's work, delicate art woven in stone. Nothing surprised you after a while. There were bricked-up doors and windows all along the walls. Alcoves, arches, and columns. A forty-foot section of floor where iron rails pierced the brick and then simply stopped beside a nonexistent loading dock. There were squat tunnels done in yellow ceramic tile like the subway, with the same black vacancy at the extremities.

It was a huge and haunted place, more like a morgue than a library. You matched your ticket numbers to the little tags hanging on every roll of cloth; then you pulled your roll out of the bin, cradling it like a child for a moment before dropping it into its shipping box, always an avalanche of dust and grime falling in your face from the dark upper bins, the paper ripping on extrusions, the cloth unraveling like torn curtains. Until after a while you could convince yourself that they really were bodies, crumbling mummies stacked in open crypts like those war atrocities.

And then I try to imagine a man like Murtaugh inside that same place for twenty years.

He was the one guy who lasted, and he looked like the fifties never ended. Every day he wore a white cotton T-shirt, jeans, and biker boots—a uniform so unvarying that I accepted it as normal after a few weeks. The hair he kept in a disciplined flattop. His eyes were pale blue pools of no particular depth. And his immense size was, in a sense, the only shape that stayed in your mind. Pardue told me that he had once served time for killing a man with a logging chain. "Don't mess with him," he said. And I did not. Murtaugh kept a Zippo lighter in his hip pocket that he flipped open with a single snap of his fingers, and he held his cigarette cupped, like this, against some imaginary hurricane. On weekends we did not visit him in the green boardinghouse on Broad Street, and on nights when they needed some overtime we did not volunteer to stay behind with him. Even during the regular shift, Murtaugh would sort through the packing slips, selecting orders that would take him to the farthest aisles, down the long tunnels, and out beyond the ordered bins where the only lights were hanging bulbs. On some nights we did not see him at the elevator drop at all.

4

Every once in a while Pardue would go off on Meek, about how he needed to be killed or at least thrown through one of the walled-up windows. "They're doing layoffs again," he would say. "And I think that asshole enjoys it. He needs killing. Did you ever notice that the personnel guy is the last one laid off?"

"I don't think he enjoys it," I said. "I think he's just doing his job."

"I'll *tell* you what he enjoys. He enjoys porking that little gal in the commissary what you been going out with, name of Patty. I hear he's been spending a lot of time down there."

I didn't say anything.

"Don't nothing rile you up, kid? You need to stomp that son of a bitch into the ground."

"Patty's not that kind of girl."

"Forget Patty! You need to kill that bastard. I'll tell you what you need."

"What do I need?"

"You need somebody . . . from West Virginia. You need a dynamite man."

"I need a dynamite man?"

"You need somebody from West Virginia, son, the Explosives State, where they mix gunpowder in your grits and a cook-off don't have nothing to do with the Pillsbury Doughboy."

"I guess you might know somebody."

"I *am* from West Virginia, boy. We got dental hygienists up there who use Primacord instead of dental floss, and when you hear a high-speed drill it don't mean your wisdom teeth are coming out, Jack. It means the whole damn side of your mountain is about to lift and slide, that's what it means. Hell, back home we got twelve-year-old boys can blow the wax out of your ears and not even wake you up during the sermon. In fact, you don't even need me. You don't need no dynamite man. You need a twelve-year-old. From back home. In West By God Virginia."

"I don't know," I said. "Maybe I don't need anybody who's from a state that's just a chopped-off part of another state."

"Now you're catching on. Hey!" he yelled out over the room. "Riggs is developing a brain! He's coming up out of the swamp! Go ahead, kid, give me your best shot."

"Like y'all ought to change your name. I mean, West Virginia's not a state, it's a direction. It makes you look small."

"It ain't ever hurt West Consin none, has it?"

"So what were you planning to dynamite?"

"Meek, I done told you. I'm going to dynamite his ass into the middle of next week."

"You're going to blow up Meek?"

"Naw. Hell naw! A hunnerd times better than that. This here's a variation on your classic cherry bomb in the toilet, except we'll probably need a couple of sticks of c4 on account of we want him riding a geyser right after he flushes."

Willie T. gave a piercing whistle and yelled, "Bring 'er on in for a minute, boys. This is going to get good."

When he had his audience, Pardue said, "We'll need to cut off the water for most of this section of the mill, you know, to build up the pressure pretty good, and then reinforce the pipe at the actual point of detonation. I want it to blow an eight-inch column of water through his butt. I want it to rocket that son of a bitch through the ceiling tiles so that his head will come through the next floor and somebody will step on him. I want it to look like he's riding Old Faithful to the moon. You understand what I'm saying? I hate that cracker! I want him to pull down his pants, take a seat, pull that damn handle, and think that he accidentally launched the space shuttle. That's what I want. And I'm telling you we can do it. It's a matter a teamwork."

"Have you ever done anything like this before?"

"Not me specifically. But I witnessed something similar back in high school. It was sad, really. Kind of tragic in a way. And it caused an international incident that you boys may have heard of, which should teach you the value of careful and strategic thinking and also something about the fragility of human life. So I reckon I'm going to have to tell you about it."

"I thought you might need to."

"Okay, there's this one old boy name of Pruitt who hated the assistant principal the way I hate Meek and who came up with something of the same plan but without careful thinking. What I'm telling you is they forgot to reinforce the sewer drain pipe at a vital point. It makes me sick to this day to think about it, and, well, you can probably already imagine what happened. Pruitt and his boys stopped up most of the toilets on the third and fourth floors and waited for the crucial moment right before the assembly where the genuine Boys Choir of Wales, I'm not making this up, was going to give its international Christmas concerto for the backward children of West Virginia, you know, on account of they thought that would be a likely time for the son of a bitch to visit the toilet. And sure enough he did. Everything was going to plan. The little Wales children was warming up backstage. Pruitt and his gang was hulking over several toilet bowls like vultures with a couple sticks of dynamite and a Bic, waiting for a miracle. And, by God, it happens. The assistant principal comes in with one of the singers, a little tiny pissant of a Wales kid name of Cardiff Glendenning it turns out, showing him where the bathroom is. Well, Pruitt and his gang are in this one stall, feet up off the floor hulking on the rim of the commode so the place looks deserted. And they hear their guy. Then they hear the stall door next to 'em close and the little lock go snick, like that; and they figure it's a go for liftoff. So Pruitt gives the nod, and ffftt goes the fuse and flush goes the charge. Fifteen seconds later there's this dull, distant boom like thunder rolling down the mountain. And, oh, sweet Jesus!"

"What happened?"

"Nothing happened," I said. "He's making this up as he goes along."

"I'm going to tell you what happened as soon as I get a grip on my stomach because it gives me the dry heaves to this very day. It makes me want to puke just thinking about it. There was a tragic miscalculation. And what happened, boys, is that one hunnerd yards downstream the pipe blew. It couldn't take the blast, see, and it was like one of them submarine movies except it was blowing high pressure sewage through that cafeteria and it was like the U-571 taking the entire eighth grade to a watery grave."

"I thought you said the entire school was in the assembly listening to the boys choir of some damn place you probably made up."

"I'm telling you they was in the cafeteria, and they was *fouled*, fouled something terrible. But that ain't the worst part. Because . . . oh my Lord, that poor little boy. You see, it was him in the toilet and not the assistant. It was horrible, just horrible."

"It blew him up?"

"No! A hunnerd times worse. In fact, the exact opposite. When that pipe blew four stories below and every drop of water in the entire system headed toward the center of the earth, what the hell you think happened? It created a suction like a hurricane blowing through your empty head. I can hear his screams to this day. And I can imagine the horror. Just think of it yourself, poor little Cardiff looking down between his legs and seeing what? A tiny ripple and then, all of a sudden, a whirlpool like the damn *Titanic* was going down. And the force of suction? Good God Almighty, boys, Superman couldn't pull himself out of a force like that. It threw his legs together and formed a perfect seal so damn fast it was foregone before it was foredone; and that ill-fated child was bent in the shape of a V and singing soprano for sure, fighting for his life, and praying 'Sweet Jesus, if you love a sinner, get me out of this American toilet.' In fact, those might have been his last words."

"His last words?!"

"That's right. What I'm trying to tell you, boys, is that young Cardiff was never seen again. And I believe to this very moment it was the tragedy that turned my life in the direction that it eventually took, ruining me for medical school or one of the higher professions. That little boy's story is in many ways identical to my own. It's why I stand before you today a broken and humble man."

"That's a damn lie!"

"It's no lie, boys. I swear on my sweet grandmaw's grave."

"It's a gah-damn lie on account of you never been inside a high school in your life."

5

When the layoffs began again, they started in the weave room and worked their way through the departments. The weavers were replaced by automated looms, inspectors by scanning machines. And the weave room went from being as noisy as a field of crows to being as silent as the grave. And the dye house lost its steam. Then I guess they sent the carding and spinning operations overseas where they weren't as particular about brown lung and wanted to share the opportunity with folks making twenty cents an hour. That's what Pardue said. He said, "Boys, you better read the handwritin' on the shithouse wall," meaning, I suppose, that we were as obsolete as John Henry's hammer. Still, I took pride in the fact that binners and pickers were the last to go, though when they came for Willie T., he simply said, "Fellas, I lost my job." Never suspecting that it may have been lost for him.

When they came for me, it was like I had done something wrong, which I guess I had in a way. I should have tried some college after all. For a time I worked security at a country-western place called Boots, where they let me try my hand at a few stand-up routines, but it never clicked. You got to make the crowds go wild if you want to do real comedy. You got to leave them gasping for air. Which I guess I never did. Within two years the mill was down to half production and only one shift. Businesses closing on Main Street while the pawn shops flourished. I got reports from my sister, who was a photographer at the local paper. She told me the mayor was applying for federal grants. Within two and a half years everyone was gone from the picking room except Murtaugh.

In my mind I could see him working alone, in his world where he had been shaped by the accumulated weight of years, dark and threatening as a thundercloud. Muscles corded under that white T-shirt like bridge cables. Hands and arms, God, like he could catch a Volkswagen if you could throw him one. Sometimes I think he had just been waiting for the rest of us to leave. Which is the way, I believe, that monsters are made. He stayed until the mill itself closed, about the same time I moved to the mountains and took up carpentry. My sister Emily sent me a picture of the picking room when it had been emptied of cloth, but it had no human perspective. It was just a photograph of a junkyard, like you could go searching the aisles forever and find nothing but the dry emptiness of canyons. And after that I tried to imagine Murtaugh walking the streets of our little town at night. Up and down, across and back, following the grid.

Jimmy John Pardue went into the movies and was arrested within a year for making the wrong kind. He bought a used video camera and a Volkswagen bus, which he drove through the mill village, offering money to girls who would accept a ride.

"Hey, sweetie, where you headed?"

And they would tell him downtown or to the movies or none of his business.

Then he would ask them, "You need a ride? Cause we can give you a ride and even give you a little money if you'll answer some questions, me and Patty here."

"What kind of questions?"

"Hop in, I'll give you forty dollars to tell us the first time you ever kissed somebody."

"What's she need a camera for?"

"That's Patty. And, Patty, I want you to meet the love of my life, the most gorgeous and most talented girl without a ride on this street whose name I want recorded right now on account of she's got the best-looking little legs I've ever seen and a smile that would stop a train. Are you Sarah? Because that's what somebody told me and you sort of look like a Sarah, you know, in a real fresh and perky kind of way. Why don't you hop in, and we'll give you a ride down to the shopping mall. I mean, if that's where you want to go. And you don't need to worry a bit. Ain't nobody going to make you take any money that you don't want to take, no sir, not one dime of this fifty dollars."

In the film that they used for evidence, there is no sound, only unsteady images of the girl herself and the occasional hand or foot of the person holding the camera. Jimmy John is at the wheel, and you can see through the windows that they are driving through the country, trees and pastures spooling by in a blur. The girl is adjusting her skirt and pulling her hair behind her ears and touching the buttons of her blouse as she answers questions from the front seat. She is smiling, handling the interview well. Relaxed and talking to the camera. At one point she giggles and leans forward, planting a mock slap on the side of Jimmy John's head. He cringes in pretend fear. And they all laugh some more. You can see the camera jiggling.

A few minutes later the girl covers her face in mock embarrassment and then answers cautiously, looking out the window at tasseled rows of corn. There's a shrug and a few more words from the front seat. Some folded twenties that get handed to the girl who stuffs them into her backpack and sits meditatively until the scene goes blank. When the light and motion resume, she is on her knees in an impossible position, her rump in the air and one shoulder and the side of her face on the floor in the middle of the van. She's smiling and talking to the camera as she lifts her skirt and tugs at the elastic of her panties. Everyone seems to be laughing and having a good time.

6

I did not marry Patty the commissary girl or play professional baseball or become a big star, but my life is all right. Today I am a wood turner in a furniture shop in the mountains where the guys say things like "Hey, Riggs, run outside and get us a tree" and I feel like I am at home. At night I lie down in a bed that I made with my own hands beside a woman named Elise who gave me the one thing that I love most in this world. And she is so tiny. Normal and perfect like her mama and as light as a snowflake in my hand. At least that is what it feels like to me.

Sometimes I tell her stories. I am still pretty good at that, and as I tell, I remember. Like how you got there by following the yellow line. One foot wide, repainted twice a year by men who never got off their knees because for them it was a never-ending line that wound through the carding room like a country road on a map. Then across the metal bridge and into the weave room where you dodged air cleaners drifting above you like jellyfish, tentacles hanging all the way to the floor and sucking up the cotton fibers so it's like the cleanest floor you've ever seen, weavers bustling around in hairnets and masks like surgeons.

Then you took the yellow stairs down. Punched through two sets of swinging doors and went down some more until you smelled vinegar or maybe heard the dyer himself slamming at a bolt with one of his wrenches. And pretty soon there he would be, sweating on account of the steam and not even wasting a glance in your direction. Most of the time you only knew him as a pair of legs and a leather apron there in the blue fog, but it would be him all right. He never left the dye house. It was like the laundry room of a prison, the air a roiling thundercloud of blue steam. But sometimes you could see him in one of the aisles between vats, where he'd be roasting like a pig, arms absolutely blue to the elbows and where, if you came close enough, you would notice the one startling fact that stayed with you all the years. That his eyes were perfectly matched to his arms, the cobalt blue of new blue jeans.

Those are the things I remember because there was no direct route into the picking room. You had to follow the painted pathway. You had to take the yellow stairs down. And once engulfed in that fog, you simply held you breath until you reached the freight elevator, which, everybody said, was a one-way drop, like the canary cage dangling from some miner's hand as he takes the long ride down. And I do not know how I got out alive.

Now I look back over my life trying to see where it went right, and I find someone four years old climbing into my lap, there in the big chair, on nights when the wind rushes up through the valley. And I try to think of what to tell her when she asks where the monsters come from.

TWO WHO DROWNED

Refiner's Fire

So many things at once. Like this.

The woman I live with is white, which for some people, I suppose, counts as an accomplishment. While for me it suggests that they must have been desperate down there, at the church. Someone must have had a vision. And someone else must have decided they needed a delegation. So you see what I mean. None of this story makes sense when you tell it straight. I'm guessing they prayed for a month before reaching the bottom of their barrel, and then they prayed some more and sent elders up here to my house, scraping and shuffling like a bunch of plantation darkies, asking me what they've just been asking, blaming it all on Jesus. Maybe the only truth is this one—that I don't have any idea of what their jumbled lives are like. Maybe somebody really did have a vision. I mean, how desperate do you have to be before you start seeing things?

That's not cynicism. I'm just tired, tired of living on the edge of chaos, images coming at you like flash cards. I'm just tired. And so I see things too.

Like it's been raining all morning. I can see that. There are puddles and rivulets. I can see that too, though now the sun sharpens every detail along our street. Parked cars are shining like new Lego blocks. And the one tree in my yard, a live oak as big as my house, is shimmering with diamonds. I just don't see the angel. I suppose I could have said Jesus doesn't give a shit about the weather and I don't believe that an angel sent you either, but that would have hurt their feelings, asked them to step outside their scope of understanding. And God knows we don't do that.

So here we are, the peculiar couple, standing on the porch watching the delegation waddle down my walk like pachyderms. Karen's holding on her hip a thin black child named Lamont, who is not my son, and she is saying to me, "Maybe you could just give it a try. For a few weeks. Until they've found a new minister."

While I'm still burning up inside. Trying to sound calm.

"Did you ever notice," I say, "that church committees—black or white, it doesn't make any difference—all look like fat, greasy beggars? Except there's not a white woman in town as fat as Hula Cole. Did you ever notice that?"

"Quinn," she says.

"You could have dragged those people straight off the streets of Calcutta, added a few tons, and got exactly the same effect. I mean, Jesus Christ, John Powell Baity looks like that fool who played Uncle Remus in the . . ."

"Quinn, nobody came here to insult you."

"Don't be so sure."

"I think you would do a wonderful job."

"I like the church the way it is, all singing and no sermon."

"They need a minister."

"They need a touch of reality. Far as I'm concerned, that pulpit can stay vacant till they find somebody from the Ku Klux Klan who'd be willing to take over for a while. What are we doing about dinner?"

"You weren't very polite while they were here."

"Look, polite to these people means yes. And in case you don't remember, I already have a job. Which is the only reason they showed up here in the first place."

"I don't think that's the only reason."

. . . and on and on and on for the next half hour until she finally smothers the flames. Like she's walking through the house turning out lights one by one, that kind of woman, who might one day save your life, or drive you insane. So let me tell you again. I'm not cynical. I'm just trying to protect what I own.

And what I'm talking about right now is a woman named Karen. Who lives with me. Wears a silver comb in her hair on most days and takes it out at night in a comforting ritual of gray-black strands shaken loose and brushed long. She does it in a way that suggests we are growing old together. And then, as she plucks off silver rings, turquoise bracelets, whatever jangly thing is around her neck, she places them in some solemn order upon her dresser as if praying for grandchildren. So I tease her. Every night. Because that's the way we say it, by looking together into the same mirror and searching for a silver comb that seems suddenly, inexplicably lost in perfect camouflage. And the long dresses, I think, simply mean that she owns an art gallery, although they still remind me of the year we met. Back then we were a revolution. Now we are only an oddity. And the sweaters? I don't know. I suppose she's just cold.

So this is a story about us. No matter what happens in between.

You should know that there are crayons scattered over the floor because the porch of my house, which is really a veranda, is wide enough and deep enough to look like an invitation to every untethered child in town. There are crayons and piles of paper, chalk and the remnants of someone's homework. There are two books fluttering like wounded birds. A pair of pink flip-flops. There's a basketball. A stack of Monopoly money in green, yellow, pink, and white but no Monopoly board and no Monopoly tokens. Only a lingering argument over the money—isn't that a surprise? And one of Karen's hairbrushes and a knotted hair band. But there's also a momentary calm, broken soon enough by one of the older boys, maybe eight or nine, with a mouth full of sass and that accusatory tone that they use to disguise hope.

He starts in on me, just after the damn committee leaves.

"How come," he says, "how come you don't never tell a story 'bout a black man?"

"I do," I say. "I've *written* stories about . . ."

But he looks at me like I'm the white principal.

"Look, I already have. Aesop was a black man. So was Lemuel Hawes. Jackie Robinson. So was Abram White."

"How come you don't tell no stories 'bout a black man living right now? That ends happy. I ain't no turtle."

"Hush now. Hush," says Karen. Patting the big one's back. Pulling little Lamont into the comfort of her, his legs dangling on either side of her hip. "Hush now." This time to Lamont. "You're not hurt anymore." And her own hair falling loose in places and the full sway of her breasts as she walks among the other children and the dangling jewelry and the smell of her. Do you see what I mean? I have no idea what their quarrel was about, and yet she's there among them, like the shepherd, and I am here on the edge, like the dog, looking for direction.

So I adjust my glasses and tug tight the cardigan she gave me for Christmas, the way I do in class when they ask impossible questions. And I put myself where I can look over the heads of the children and down the street where another, entirely different crowd is gathering, suddenly and inexplicably. It's like the echo of the turmoil already around us. And I'm wondering if you understand yet. Because my stomach, already tightening, realizes that there is another story, a real and urgent one, unfolding farther down the hill and that I am being drawn into it at a most inconvenient spot. I'm being pulled in again because one silly, senseless event is always tied to another, that's what I've learned. And this new one at the end of my street, at the bottom of my hill, on a Sunday afternoon is far more serious than the commotion on my porch.

"How come you don't just make up a story?" says the same boy.

"Listen," I say. "There's something happening."

"Quinn . . . ," now she's trying to sound like my wife. "Do you think you ought to go?"

And I give her the same glare that the kid gave me.

"I just thought you might go look. I mean, if the police . . . Maybe you could talk to someone."

"I'm not the mayor of Coloredtown," I tell her. "I just live here, same as you. And besides, whatever it is, they don't want me in the middle of it."

Which is more than enough to send her inside with little Lamont and two of the girls, saying thin-lipped the way she does, "Come along now," like she thinks I can do something about every drunk who smacks his wife on the weekend. Seventeen years and she still doesn't realize I have a history with these people. That I wear cardigan sweaters for God's sake and steel-rimmed glasses. That I teach literature, Karen, the first black man at Baxter College who doesn't push or pull something. And so of course they don't trust me. I don't even speak their language. I've grown used to the money. I sit on committees. How can she live with me for seventeen years and not realize?

But here I am, aren't I, on the damp sidewalk looking back at my empty porch. The children have scattered like biddies, and here I am looking back at a wide, smiling veranda that makes my house look like a plantation house. Rattan chairs big enough for kings. And ferns on either side of the door set like African headdresses on white fern stands. And a brick walkway that leads up to gray porch steps. So we say out loud that it's a porch, but we've made it, after all these years, into the one untroubled crossroads of our town where once, long ago, I sat jamming with a group of musical men who laughed and played half the night. That's what I'm mad about. She can slam the damn door all she wants.

Because who you are determines where you live in Baxter. And I mean where you sit and stand. Professors in one part of town, businesspeople in another. Black folks over here on the hill. Which is how

I've come to be walking down toward my neighbors who are gathering around the echoes of gunshots and the sound of a distant siren and now, suddenly, another. Because something has happened again. At first it doesn't seem real to me without television commercials and the cool, flat flickering images. But here I am walking down my own street beneath the bare dripping limbs of willow oaks, wiping my glasses with a handkerchief and muttering to myself like a tourist lost in some insane, chattering marketplace. Even though I live in a hundred-year-old house. As close to the campus as you can get without crossing tracks.

So I walk, and it's like descending into a dream. The Jamaican lawn ornaments, the painted doorways. Like she sent her voice to follow me into dreamland, only an octave higher; and I know before I look. It's that boy who can't keep himself from beneath my feet or shut his mouth long enough to breathe. Saying, "How come you don't be the new preacher?" Just out of reach and as insistent as a mosquito. "You could preach, couldn't you? Ain't that what you already do?"

"I try not to."

"Why not?"

"Why don't you tell me what your name is."

"I stay with my aunt sometimes, Lamont's mama." The inflection rising as if this were a question. "I watch him till supper time most days."

"That's not what I asked you, is it?"

"James Lee Kenrick. What you do for money?"

"I teach at the college, James Lee Kenrick. And besides . . . you don't just wander in off the street and start preaching. Whether there's a vacancy or not."

"Sometimes you do. I seen it happen."

But I walk ahead of him, down the hill, beneath cathedral-columned oaks and into the ruin of our neighborhood where two streets cross.

When we reach the edge of the crowd, we stay there, on the margin of a tragedy that's been gathering for days. I think I can guess, but it takes

Silvia to confirm it. She is Lonell's mother. More police arrive and then an ambulance, and I'm taken into the swirl of bodies as the crowd gets jostled to one side and then another while yellow crime-scene tape goes up around the tree. Over the ditch. Across the car. Down to the hedge and back over the driveway. Then a black cop and a white cop are working together to push the crowd back. Nightsticks out and up, like this, pushing the people back into the street. But it's Silvia that I see with electric clarity, not the building chaos around me. Silvia with wild hair and frantic flying hands. Two women who are trying to hold her up, but she keeps throwing herself to the ground, tearing at the grass, her clothes, and shrieking louder than sirens. Because it's Lonell in the ditch, under the blue blanket; and several men have come out of the crowd to help her. While I'm thinking, God, what have we done now? But of course I already know.

I can see them behind me and to my right, three teenagers in warm-ups, as dignified as old men. Practicing their nonchalance, but managing nevertheless to lurch like vultures until one of them finally breaks a smile. "They put that mug under a blue blanket, man. *Blue!*" Like it was the final insult. "Gonna *bury* that mu'fucker in it. Serve him right!" One of them snickering. One of them staring cold hate.

And on the ground beside the tactful blanket is a policeman and another policeman straddling his chest, pumping with desperate jolts that shake his jowls. A pistol in the grass. Someone's shoe. And more sirens in the distance. More flashing lights as paramedics arrive for the wounded cop and lift him into the first ambulance without a glance at the crumpled blanket and then try to drive away. Lonell motionless all this time, the fingers of one hand dug into the dirt as if at the moment of death his greatest fear had been falling away from the earth. While some people in the crowd have begun shouting at the outsiders, blocking the path of the ambulance because official Baxter has left behind another black boy, like garbage. Two state patrol cars now, both troopers grim and gray, moving the people out of the street and into adjoining yards. A fat teenage girl shrieking, "I hate white people!"

But of course white people didn't kill Lonell Burns. And when I turn and look for James Lee Kenrick I see that he too is gone, lost somewhere in the crowd.

It's a story that's over before I arrive. A distant horrifying fantasy. Now someone will have to write about it, explain it, translate it. And it's at this moment that I go sick and drop myself onto Baity's white brick wall and pansies, because I know who will take it up and what she will say long before she knows herself. One of those reporters, one of those stick-thin girls graduated from the college, maybe one I've taught myself, as white as desert sand and as breathless and sincere as Jane Austen, and about as prepared for the cough-cough of a Glock 9 mm. Who, sometime this evening, will begin writing about life among the lowly, death in a ditch, for tomorrow's newspaper. Poor Jane, she will be, who will let seep between her words an unconscious amazement that we are human beings. As though we were put on this planet to be discovered. And poor us, who will read and watch the television reports not recognizing anyone, least of all ourselves, as the story trickles out.

So some will rant like the fat girl. And some will scratch our heads. Because the newspaper will say a normally peaceful neighborhood. The tranquility of early evening shattered by gunfire. A troubled teen. The irony that Lonell's own family called the police, trying to prevent bloodshed. That Officer McLane himself would be the first to die.

Then on the day after irony there will appear a second story with numbers, this one written by a feature writer from the city paper twenty-five miles away who will not add an ounce of understanding. It will say three sisters, one cousin, five rooms, and three generations in a modest dwelling on Mott Street. Ten years of schooling, eight suspensions, and several incidents. A total of twelve grams stolen from the dealer earlier in the week, three gold necklaces, and a 9 mm. And taken from Lonell in retaliation: one girlfriend, one child. Then six days between incidents. Three shots fired at Lonell in the drive-by. But no injuries. Seven minutes before Lonell can get his cousin to safety and return home for the gun. Five people who try to restrain him. Two policemen who respond to the call. One can of Mace. One scuffle on the ground. One gathering crowd. One person to reach out of the crowd and pull McLane's arm away. And a horrible, ironic twist to the plot: three shots by Lonell striking McLane in the neck and face. Then two shots by the second cop from point-blank range. For a grand total of ninety-seven.

It's how they see the world.

Then I will pass the first one on the street, the girl with the sincere pencil, and she will want some words from me, the symbolic spokesman for the tongue-tied class. Because she will think I am safe and sadly white. And she will fumble for her notebook as I take down my glasses, draw out a handkerchief, and squint. Holding the lenses up to the sun like a boy burning ants, thinking furiously. How can I hate this girl who is true to her way of knowing and not hate myself, who could have told a lie nine years ago and prevented myself from observing, "It's a tragedy." As I examine her through the one smudged lens and fit the frames back over deaf ears. And hear myself say, "A painful moment for us all."

Still in the muddle of it, I walk back up the hill thinking of Homer. The Greek poet, yes, in this unlikely place. The Homer who could easily have imagined the grim and gratified young men who provoke death, though they could not have imagined him. I'm trying to remember details, but I suspect Karen has been on the phone already with that circle of women who manage things late at night when the knock comes, the dark man on the front porch with a flashlight. And she'll be quietly waiting for whatever words I can put. She'll ask me what happened, meaning something entirely different from the words. And I will say all those young men, Karen. All those young men, who stab each other at the ships, will come back tomorrow with different names and precisely the same quarrels—you disrespected me, took my woman, walked upon my turf. You touched my golden chain, struck my child. You prey upon my waking thoughts and steal my sleep. I don't even think they want the monster dead. They want a poet rapping ancient lines, another someone who will translate for them. But right now, as I walk up the long slope, they step out of the early evening fog and into the place where I imagine them, the dark, moist dreamland where they are

> churning around that ship, Achaeans and Trojans,
> hacking each other at close range. No more war at a distance,
> waiting to take the long flights of spears and arrows—
> they stood there man-to-man and matched their fury,
> killing each other now with hatchets, battle-axes,
> big swords, two-edged spears, and many a blade,
> magnificent, heavy-hilted and thonged in black
> lay strewn on the ground—some dropped from hands,
> some fell as the fighters' shoulder straps were cut—
> and the earth ran black with blood.

Something I could have taught them.

So finally I sag into a kitchen chair, and she reaches out across the table to take my hands in hers before drawing away for coffee. Then slides a steaming cup beneath my face. And I inhale. It's like incense wafting across the face of some hollow idol.

"What happened?" is all she can think to say.

"What happened? They don't even know themselves."

"A drive-by?"

"It doesn't make any difference. Next year it'll be someone else," I tell her. "That baby you held this afternoon will kill somebody trying to become a man. Fast or slow, it doesn't make any difference. In fact I believe my friend Lonell might have come out a winner considering that he never had a chance."

"He had a choice."

"White people have a choice. Lonell had the world he lived in. So why don't you ask me what the rest of them really want to know—where was the boy's father? Where was some thick-muscled man to knock him back from the edge? Where do they all go?"

She looks at me the way she does when we are strangers—it happens from time to time—though in seventeen years we've never fought, not once. Never a hateful word between us. People are amazed. We just draw back. She on her side of the track, me on mine, until one of us figures a way across. It's where we are now. She's sipping her own coffee, stirring with a cinnamon stick and thinking. Combing her hair back with her fingers. Twirling the ring on her finger. Until finally, "I've never seen you this down before. You must have known him, known his family." Her face a perfect oval of concern.

I say to her, "Did you know I grew up in this town? Played in this very house when I was a boy because it belonged to my grandmother Miss Ginny who built it before there was a track. Whose money sent me up north to school and brought me back here to . . . whatever it is. It's almost beyond comprehension. Did you know my real name was *Quinthony*? Not Quentin. But Quinthony. Quinthony Hodges Deagan. It's one of those black names, like Lakeesha or Gonorrhea Jones."

"Stop it."

My face falls down into my hands, and some low moaning sound comes forth. "We need to quit pretending. You and I. We need to quit pretending that we're horrified by these stories. I mean we can at least be honest, right? That's what we have instead of hope."

Then she is there at my shoulders, the hair and the scent of her. Kneading the muscles the way she takes up clay and reaches into the being of it before throwing it on the wheel. "I'll see you in hell first," she whispers in my ear. "I'll drag you back a hundred times. You have no idea how far I'll go. Now tell me—what really happened?"

And since there are only two of us in a house fit for a family, and since she is strong, I say, "Let me ask you a question."

Suppose you can't sleep because you have the same dream every night— that it's been raining and that there are puddles and rivulets, diamonds and toys scattered about, and the Angel Malachi waiting for you at the end of a long walk. And that he is tall and patient. Thin as a mantis and hungry for souls. But you don't want to see him. You say to yourself this is a dream, and I am an educated man, and that is just some old fellow who hands out Bibles. One of those homeless who stand outside the gates of the college thrusting little green testaments at anyone who passes, while cars go hissing past even though his trench coat, shiny wet and chitinous, stretched tight against his wings, glistens with liquid light. His hands hooked over a Bible and eyes, yes, burning like brimstone.

Until you have to remind yourself that what you're seeing is not real.

But in this particular dream the Angel Malachi will be examining several versions of you because he has eyes like a dragonfly and because one version of you goes blundering through a maze like a blind man. And so he puts himself at a place where your paths converge and says, "This really isn't very complicated."

Though of course you misunderstand. You go as stiff as a corpse and say, "Good God Almighty! Jesus, mister, you shouldn't come up on a man like that." As the angel closes his eyes. Waits. And you stammer on a step or two hoping to leave him behind by saying, "Look, pal, I don't have anything on me. I left my wallet back at the . . . I don't have a nickel."

And the angel says, "It's not that kind of hunger."

Which provokes some cheap fear from you like, "What do you want? Just tell me what you want."

And the Angel Malachi says, "What do we always want?"

So that's what I'm asking you.

If you don't believe in the Walt Disney of it, Karen, then what does he want? If you can't stomach the fried chicken of it, if you can't stand in

front of them shouting, "Thank you, Jesus," for crabgrass and aluminum
siding, then what the hell does he want? Because I can't go back to Bible
stories. Not after Lonell and the rest of them.

On the patio she finds me after two days with that hanging question, and I'm feeding the books into the fire because I've finally made the decision they wanted me to make. I'll give them three weeks. And they'll probably take everything that I own. I believe that's the usual deal.

The fireplace huffs and bellows when the wind whirls, drawing the ashes up like dark confetti, the end of a long process of decomposition. And I've noticed *this*. That first a sheet of paper will crumple in upon itself as if crushed by an invisible hand; and then it will quiver and fall apart, not like rich pine that sizzles in its own juice and then explodes, but like a mummy under eager examination, though of course sometimes it simply smolders, has to be prodded into flames with the poker; and then there is a rush of fire, thick runnels of red and orange that lick halfway up the chimney. Then something like snowflakes, huge three-inch floaters that can be caught in the palm and read. It's unbelievable but true. The words are not gone at all. You can still read them.

So I burn Bradbury first, that old standby. Then *Light in August*. Then Tolstoy. Then Milton and Melville together, pages curling up like people in pain. It's surprising really, how much heat there is in old books. I have to wait a moment until I can add *Huckleberry Finn*. Mary Shelley. Leaves going red and blue at the margins, yellow-orange at the center like the flames themselves. Some of the steel print engravings send up a green leafy blaze, from the chemicals I suppose. And pale loose pages fly upward, scattering like quail until they burst into a brilliance I've never seen in the classroom, then spiral down on wings of fire. There's no denying it's beautiful. No matter what you feel, there's no denying the beauty of it. I'm seeing what the Nazis saw. And tomorrow I'll feel what I feel. That's tomorrow. But right now . . . There's much more heat than we realize. I have to lift my hand momentarily and back away. Then stir the ashes. Then add a thin one, a bright blue one by Anne Frank.

The weight of it is almost too much to bear.

Then I sense her beside me, Karen, looking into my mirrored eyes and crying, "Oh my God! Oh Jesus no! Quinn, what are you doing?!"

And I have to calm her of course. I say, "Don't worry. It runs in my family. We always destroy the evidence. We've done it for generations. My great-grandfather. My grandmother Miss Ginny. She once burned an entire house and then built a new one, then married a custodian who worked at the college for over . . ."

"Quinn, please don't, please."

"It's all right," I say. "It's all right. They can't imagine it, our neighbors. They can't even imagine me. They think we're burning trash."

With her arms around me now. Trying to squeeze the life back into me, work the same silly miracle that they want to work when they lift their sons' shoulders off the sidewalk and feel the warm blood beneath. Birth-fluid seeping into the soil while they become oblivious to every other need of the universe. That kind of woman. Who'll fight right up to the gates of hell. Telling me, and the world, with all her strength. That love is God.

I don't hate the books. I know them as intimately as I know the angry-frightened woman clutching the shawl, who refuses to be warmed by abstractions. "Listen to me," she is saying. "You're not anything until I love you. I don't understand this, Quinn. You're brilliant. You're successful. You're kind and generous. You and I—right now—are where the world wants to be in fifty years, or a hundred. I'm not going to let that go."

"So why can't I just be content?"

"No. Why can't you realize you're not responsible for every broken child?"

It takes a while, but finally I tell her, shove aside the cardboard box and sit cradling Ralph Ellison in my hands.

"Because I could have saved him. Once upon a time."

"I don't believe that."

"I knew his mother, Silvia, before I knew you. He must have been five or six when I first met her, a bit older when we drifted apart."

"You don't have to do this."

"Anyhow, I remember one night, just after there was you, sitting out on that porch and jamming with some of the folks from down the way. It seemed so natural then, simply spreading out over the porch and busting some old tunes. Beer in a tub of ice, mosquitoes getting blown back by all that sweet sound, just letting the music take us wherever it would. Must have been six or eight of us with old pawned-up instruments we'd pulled out of the closet. Maybe one or two fellows with some real talent, but it didn't make any difference. Just some old men with some old songs. James Teague, you know him, sitting on the edge of a rocker blowing trumpet. Some guy named Perry on bass. Harmonica man on the steps, me with that old Gibson thinking I was B. B. King. They had even rolled the piano over into the doorway, and I was thinking, man, this is the way it ought to be.

"I don't want to make it out to be something wild. It wasn't. There was plenty of quiet talk in between the notes, joking and carrying on. One or two couples standing in the yard. Maybe somebody dancing, but nothing rowdy enough that you'd notice from the street, or even remember. Just folks unwinding from the day, trying to ease on into tomorrow. That's all. But it must have looked like a mob to a nine-year-old.

"When the train rumbled by, we didn't try to compete; we just laid back and let it roll; and I remember letting my eyes drift down the walk to this boy who'd been standing at the outermost edge of the light. Dressed in a white shirt and Sunday pants like somebody'd told him it was a church night. Then walking toward me during the rattle and clang of the train. I knew he was Silvia's boy. And I knew it must have taken everything he had. Waiting for the train to pass, then whispering into the sudden silence, in that accusatory tone they use when there's still hope, 'Somebody said you was my daddy.'

"'Whoa-ha!' says the bass man. 'Here it come!'

"But there was nothing else, just some quiet laughter and this boy. And, for a long time, me. The funny thing is that I didn't even have to lie. I just said, 'Son, I'm not your father. Somebody told you wrong.' Which was the thing that subtracted him down to tears."

She waits for me to finish, but there isn't anymore. I love this house. The books. The woman. I'm just trying to make room. That's the only story I have to tell.

When he was little, Lonell played basketball in my driveway, a loose-packed gravel ramp to nowhere that made it a pass and shoot game. Back then it looked like a sharecropper's field. Your feet went pounding through ruts, crackle and pop, with the ball taking wild crazy bounces that made little white boys want to cry. They all said it, over and over and over. No blood, no foul. You had to bump and go. You had to turn and shoot into the sun. That's what they learned from the age of nine. You had to earn that smooth level blacktop down at the schoolyard. You had to be recruited to play on the playground. And that's why I remember his face. Pain and joy twisted into one fierce effort that made it obvious where he wanted to go.

Pulp Life

At the final hearing, the one where the sentence was set, my judge said he wanted to find justice. That is the phrase he used. And, of course, my parents wanted me at home. That is what the parents always want, although I am convinced that they would have said anything to keep me there. They answered eagerly as the distracted judge, looking for misplaced justice, set forth the provisions. But I do not know what Mrs. Anders wanted. Perhaps her son back. She was a dark and quiet woman who had spent the entirety of her life on a farm just outside our town. Her son had been her only accomplishment; and when it came time for her to hand over the photograph, she walked it to the bench as if she were carrying a wounded bird.

Years later, in the front bedroom of what used to be my parents' house, this same judge said to me that there is never justice in cases like mine. That it's never found. The sentence is at best a ragged fiction. "You simply try to ruin as few lives as possible," he mused. But on the day of that final hearing he went searching for justice, shuffling through papers until he seemed to find it in a moment of inspiration. The only other people in the courtroom on that day were the reporter who wrote the story, an assistant district attorney named Harris, a court recorder, and my own lawyer, who, you might have thought, would have said something. Or maybe she was just thinking what my parents were thinking. That I had just got lucky.

First, however, before my judge went searching among his papers and patting the folds of his robe, he asked me what I remembered. And I said that I did not remember the accident itself because I had been drinking and that I did not remember the hospital because I had been unconscious. Perhaps I did realize at some level that I had been driving and that Jackie and Andrea were both there with me because I could still recall their voices over the deep bass of the music. That night when time stopped. But I did not remember the road or the lights. It was all just a splash of color and pain.

"At least you're honest," he said. "What about today, Miss Meyer, do you expect you'll remember that?" He called me Miss Meyer, I think, because I was seventeen or maybe because he wanted to make a point, since he called my attorney Ms. McBryde and he called Mrs. Anders Mrs. Anders. Those are the details that I remember now, not the actual sentencing but the very beginning of that afternoon when he said to me, "What about today, Miss Meyer, do you think you'll remember that?" And I did: the numbness in my fingers, the dry, shallow breathing, and the chill along my legs, all as if he had found what he had been looking for on the far planes of an arctic desert.

I cried back to everyone, "I'm so sorry, I don't know what I can do or what I can say," finally breaking down, not realizing that my body could shake that hard. Ms. McBryde holding me up with one arm. And when my father reached for me, the judge told him to sit down. So I don't know how long it was before I could hear again. Sometimes I think it's still going on, that moment, right now. In the future.

". . . me ask you about the victim. Do you remember him at all?"

"I didn't see him. I didn't even see his truck," I said. "I didn't realize there was an intersection until my arms broke, that's the other thing I can remember, and I'm so sorry and I just want Mrs. Anders to know that. . . ."

"Address the court, Miss Meyer. Don't speak to anyone else but your attorney."

"I just wanted her to know."

"She already knows, Miss Meyer. It doesn't help."

"I'm so sorry. I just . . ."

"Okay, let's wind this up. Ms. McBryde, do you have anything else?"

"No, Your Honor."

"Mr. Harris?"

"No, Your Honor."

"Okay. Okay, that'll do it. Let's get this . . . Where's that other form? No, the plea agreement, the one before that other one. It's already gone down? Okay, let me see the one for this one. Okay. Okay, good, that's what I need. Let's get this one in the hopper. Get this one—where's my pen?—in the hopper. All right. Miss Meyer, there are two types of felony DWI in this state, the habitual offender statute and death by motor vehicle while intoxicated. You've been charged and you have pled guilty to violation of the second of these statutes, and the court has heard statements from your attorney, from Mr. Harris, and from the family of the deceased. In considering your sentence the court has taken note that you are a minor child, living at home, with no previous convictions and thus with prospects of a long, useful, and even rewarding life. But the court has also taken note that the victim, Mr. Anders, was planning to be married and did himself look forward to a full and happy life as breadwinner, husband, and father. It is this latter prospect that you have taken away. Your reckless disregard has reached far beyond one life, Miss Meyer, and in dealing with an adult offender I would ordinarily offer a sentence of seven to twenty years confinement. In this case, however, I see nothing but senseless waste and pain associated with every aspect. I've taken into consideration your admission of guilt, your obvious remorse, and the very gracious and compassionate statement by the Anders family. In accord with all those things, I hereby sentence you to fourteen years supervised proba-tion, permanent revocation of your driver's license, participation in an alcohol treatment program to be approved by your supervisor, and this additional provision—that from this day until the end of your stated probation, with no exception, appeal, or extenuation, you be required to carry upon your person a photograph of the deceased as a perpetual reminder of the consequences of your actions. If at any time, twenty-four hours a day, seven days a week, your probation supervisor finds that you are not in physical possession of this photograph, he or she will report so to this court, and an immediate sentence of five to seven years confinement in the state penal system will be ordered. Do you understand the provisions of this sentence?"

"Yes, Your Honor."

"Ms. McBryde, you've covered all this with them?"

"Yes, Your Honor."

"Good. So ordered. Mrs. Anders, have you selected the photograph in accordance with our previous conversation?"

"Yes, Your Honor."

"Would you bring it forward please."

Amazing Stories, **November 1939, Volume 13, Number 11.** $47. Cover illustration by H. W. McCauley. Lead story "The Four-Sided Triangle" by William F. Temple. Other stories by Ralph Milne Farley, Robert Moore Williams, Frederic Arnold Kummer Jr., and Don Wilcox. Overall G to VG condition. Cover background now fading to violet with magenta undertones — originally a sharp medium blue (see other copies of A.S. from the 1930s). No splits or tears. All pages intact. Minor flaking and chipping where cover overlaps the pages beneath. Cash purchase at Second Foundation.

What drew me to this one was the color work. The individual letters of the words *Amazing Stories* are bright yellow, rising off the page like an old movie title. A thin russet outline gives the lettering dimension but also tricks the eye into seeing molten gold rather than crayon yellow. It is a startling effect to someone who has not been spoiled by Star Wars. McCauley's illustration features a girl in a one-piece bathing suit, unconscious, reclining at about twenty-five degrees on a narrow platform inside a transparent capsule. Next to her is another capsule inside of which is a portion of another girl. The second girl appears to be identical to the first, but only her face and breasts are complete; the rest of her is skeleton. She is either being duplicated from the first girl or else being deconstructed by a process not made clear in the illustration. At the bottom of the picture is a figure with his back to the viewer, intently studying the encapsulated girls, one hand on the lever of a glowing machine. The light being reflected from every surface in the painting varies from the pure yellow of *Amazing Stories* to the soft orange of the instrument dials to the lurid lime-gold glow streaming from the lid of each capsule. The shading is not subtle by current standards but is blended with a technical skill I have not seen on any other cover from the 1930s.

The girl in the painting, the complete girl, does not appear to be in pain. Her bathing suit is russet with yellow highlights at her breasts and pubis. It is of course a reversal of the title's color and shading. Her skin is golden white. Her hair is golden red. The whole figure, I think, is a visual pun. Although I could not find the phrase "golden girl" in the dictionary, I believe it is a variant of "golden boy," made familiar in 1937 as the title of a Clifford Odets play and then made famous as a 1939 movie starring William Holden and Barbara Stanwyck. Both of the girls on this cover are golden girls, although only one of them has flesh.

There are two machines at the bottom of the page framing the man and making him small. They are primitive and industrial by today's standards but must have looked "scientific" to the artist McCauley. In the far background of the painting are the suggestions of other capsules and other girls, maybe rows of them, filling a huge gothic space. It is a hypnotic and horrifying moment, and I do not think this golden girl will ever escape alive.

This was my first one. I found it in a science fiction bookshop close to the campus where my parents were taking the tour. I said I would wait for them right here because, secretly, I knew there would be no going away for me. So they took the tour. And I stayed as quiet and alert as a mouse. It is still my favorite one.

My body may have remembered things that my mind could not retrieve. I think it must have remembered the impact, because at certain times during that first year it would jerk itself into rigid imitation of the russet girl with yellow highlights. Even today I can be walking around the corner of a building and be stunned by someone veering close to me. I can feel the force of our collision even though we never touch. My face being pressed against their glass. My arms, I know, will snap like toothpicks if I raise them. And I gasp, not because I am surprised, but because it is the body's lust for air. People will think that I am terrified by small things, but I am not. It's the body trying to protect itself. Back then it was still fighting to stay alive. It absorbed the impact so that my mind could continue on.

During the first year I did not ride in any automobile except my parents'. I did not go to movies. I did not buy new clothes and did not wear those given to me as presents. I did not watch television, cut my hair, or talk on the phone. On weekends I did not come out of my room. And during the week I walked to school, held my eyes like this and my arms like this. Made A's in everything. Lost twenty-two pounds in twenty-two weeks. Lost my house keys, crying with unstoppable joy at the relief of any minor tragedy. I wore dresses and cardigan sweaters in the winter, like a tourist from another country, and fell in love with the sweet oblivion of snow, sinking my hands into the powdered vapor until they burned.

During the second year, I graduated from high school, did not march across the stage, and realized the weight of the anchor holding me fast. I could have gone to any college, legally could have gone to the campus where my parents took the tour; but Gerry kept me home. In the picture he looks like my high school sweetheart, almost handsome, smiling, in the hammock, ankles crossed and hands behind his head in a way that told you he never lounged between trees except in pictures, never wasted a moment by lying still. And I looked so long I could hear him laugh. His fiancé moved to Portland with a boy who played the kind of music Gerry loved. She couldn't mourn forever. But Gerry has blue eyes and black hair that you can still see in Edinburgh, my mother said, come down from the hills and the homes where parents look suspiciously on city life. And his own mother's nose and lips. He is wearing a chambray shirt with sleeves three-quarters rolled and jeans as faded as November. It is a picture with no cuts, creases, or folds. No crumbling at the edge or split along the spine. The background is as sharply focused as his face—grass and twigs and trunk. And the condition is very good to fine. Except for the pit of my stomach where something insistent calls to me, like a baby turned to stone.

In the third year we reconciled. I went to shopping malls, enrolled at the community college. I told myself that any kind of marriage could go sour and that I was getting ahead, making myself into an independent woman, maybe a business executive one day. I took accounting, figured taxes, and filed the forms for our neighbors, who said it to my parents over and over, "I wish we had one like that at home. You're so lucky to have her in your golden years." And then one spring enrolled in a creative writing course, where they gave a solid, unshakeable A for anything. Like when he asked the class for a quick list, off the top of our heads, of things that would determine our main character's actions. And I wrote "Ten Reasons She Should Not Open Her Wallet."

1. At some point it will fall open to the unexpected place.
2. Even when she cannot see him, he is there. She is pregnant with his weight, and it is more than one woman can bear.
3. She doesn't have a right to be happy. No one does.
4. Her mother or her sister or her father will see it and start to cry. They will put their arms around her and only make it worse. One day her own child might see it, and then what?

5. She cannot wear blue because he is wearing blue.
6. In prison, the prison carries you.
7. If she keeps it closed, then he might be alive, living in a world she's never seen. And she must look for him in newspapers and magazines.
8. Every time she opens it she must pay.
9. His mother chose it. Maybe it was the only one she had. Maybe she walked it to the bench as if she were carrying a wounded bird.
10. One day it will be the oldest photograph she owns, soiled and creased like a high school picture of her husband. And someone will say, "Oh Jess, who is this?" but that is not what she hears. What she will hear instead is, "Oh Jesus, who is this?"

Which is pretty good, pretty good, the instructor said. Except maybe give her a little more depth and, you know, variety in the story so it won't sound like an obsession or one of those love poems written by a thirteen-year-old. You know what I mean?

Famous Fantastic Mysteries, April 1947, Volume 8, Number 4. $24. Cover illustration by unknown artist. Lead story "Allan and the Ice-Gods: A Journey into the Dawn of History" by H. Rider Haggard. Overall Fair to G condition. Cover background dark green to black. Spine split one inch from bottom. Slight tears and creasing at cover overhang. All pages intact, paper creamy white to light yellow. No tape or marks. Purchased through eBay.

This is another high-contrast cover with a bright yellow splash containing the title Famous FANTASTIC Mysteries in crimson. The illustration takes up two-thirds of the cover, and two-thirds of the illustration consists of an ice monolith inside of which is a frozen woman. She is reclining slightly, her eyes closed like Sleeping Beauty, and she is dressed in a long negligee or, more likely, a gown similar to those worn by Greek goddesses in the costume dramas of the 1940s and '50s. She has platinum blonde hair, full lips that might be parted for a kiss,

and breasts that prefigure Jayne Mansfield. The monolith itself is mul-
tifaceted and tinged with a green glow, although the woman's image
is undistorted.

And the hook is this: a man is kneeling at her side. He is dressed in a
leopard skin and is perhaps one-tenth the size of the woman. His head
is bowed in despair and his arms reach out to touch the surface of the
ice in a gesture of love and hopeless longing. You can tell that the man
is one-tenth the size of the woman because he is kneeling in the palm
of a giant skeletal hand, also frozen in ice. It is unclear whether the
man has been lifted to the height of the woman's breasts or whether he
climbed up the body of the giant skeleton.

This is the illustration that prompted me to make it a collection, the
covers I mean. I realized I had seen this one before, or one very much
like it, on another pulp magazine. It took me a long time to find the
original, an August 1937 cover for *Horror Stories* (volume 5, number 4)
done in pastels by John Newton Howett, where the woman is being
frozen in a transparent vat of water. She is nude, her hands pressing
against the lid of the vat as the water rises. The thermometer is below
zero. A man is leaning over her looking down as he turns the dial of a
machine. In the background are three other women who have already
been frozen.

The same story, I think, is being told on the cover of *Astonishing Stories*, November 1941: the frozen woman is being guarded by a dragon.
The same in *Planet Stories*, Summer 1948: a man and an alien are
fighting in the background. The same in *Marvel Science Stories*, April
1939: other women are looking on as the woman is being frozen. One
of them is a nurse.

I collected them, all of them that I could find over the next months.
I called it the Frozen Beauty cover because the girl isn't just sleeping and the spell cannot be broken by a kiss. Before I graduated from
high school I had collected over a hundred of the old pulps, rotting
like corpses in dim rooms of my parents' house. At yard sales or estate
clearances, I sometimes had to buy entire boxes of pulps in order to

get the one I needed. That's how it grew, became more than a collection, I suppose. One day I heard my mother fretting to the man she married, and he, like the clueless king, said, "Oh well, at least it keeps her off the street."

Time means nothing in stories like these. One day, I don't know exactly when, he simply walked into the shop as I was arranging a window display. Perhaps it was in the eleventh year, perhaps the twelfth, and at first I thought he was looking for books. He worked the maze of shelves so slowly that he seemed to be lingering over every title in the "Americana" section, then fingering the spines in "Law" as if reading them in Braille. He went through "Nature" and "Photography" just as slowly but finally returned to me after wandering through "Religion." He wore a dark wool overcoat glistening with rain droplets along the shoulders and sleeves. And in one hand he carried a gray fedora that had gone out of style in the forties. He was taller than I remembered and thin enough to make me think of my own father just before he had died.

At the pulp counter he stopped—they all do—and studied the covers, looking, I suppose, for some particular author or remembering the way the future was. "My God," he said, "I didn't know these still existed. When I was a boy, I read nearly . . ."

"I'm sorry, those aren't for sale," I said.

"Ah. Well. Do you mind if I sit down in one of these? My old knees seem to creak a bit on days when the weather . . ."

"There's coffee on the stove. Muffins next to the microwave. Please let me know if I can find something for you."

"Thank you. Yes, thank you, it's miserable out there, miserable even for this time of year, and you've made this such a lovely sanctuary, I do believe it's more inviting than the public library. Run by committees, you know. They're awful things, all of them. This must have been someone's home before you . . ."

"It was. *Is* there something I can find for you?"

He laid his hat on the coffee table I keep among the chairs and then pressed his palms together in a thoughtful moment. So I waited, the two of us together again in the front bedroom of my parents' house, a cash register and display case where the bed had stood. "I hardly know how to answer that, Miss Meyer. I don't suppose you have any recollection at all of whom I might be."

"Your name," I said, "is Burrelle. Judge Saxby Burrelle. If I remember correctly."

"Yes, retired actually. Or, rather, semiretired, I suppose you should say." He spoke in single words and phrases, like a man who has spent the last of his energy in an uphill race. "You know, I have a great-granddaughter, Miss Meyer, whom I haven't seen. In five years. I doubt she would recognize me with the perspicacity that seems to be your defining trait. There. I believe I have completed an entire thought. Without interruption."

"Judge Burrelle, if you've come here about . . ."

"Please. This will take a few moments, but I thought I should do this one in person since it involved one of my own cases. Seems the right thing, don't you agree, when one is contemplating how close he is to final judgment himself. Yes. Yes, I hadn't thought of that, consciously, until just now. One wants to do. Whatever one can."

He went on to explain that he had retired two years after hearing my case. His wife had died, and so had the partners in his old firm. And the idea of making new friends, at his age, seemed as repellent as learning how to eat new food. As he talked, I began to watch his hands the way I would have watched the hands of a child. They seemed to be more expressive than his words, cleaning his glasses with the pocket handkerchief, adjusting the fastidiously tied bow tie, checking, one by one, the buttons of his vest to make sure he had not missed a hole. I could imagine him in the first years of his emptiness learning how to tie flies, sitting up late at night in his study, peering through a magnifying glass as he twisted feathers and fur and fishing line into fantastic shapes that disguised the hook. Then lifting each one with tiny tweezers, inspecting it in the light of a goosenecked lamp. That was the way I imagined him, and it was, in a sense, the message he had come to deliver.

"After a few years," he said, "I found I couldn't stand the void, being locked in my own house twenty-four hours a day. And of course with the constant backlog of cases, tort reform, legislative review—they're glad to see anything in a black robe. So. Here I am, Miss Meyer. Here. I am."

"I'm afraid I don't understand."

"Yes. I suppose you don't. Let me ask you something first. Are you married, Miss Meyer? Is that still your name? Because this," he made a peculiar gesture with his hand, as if introducing himself to an unfamiliar audience, "is still the address of record for your case, and it's not a house at all. It's a bookstore that used to be a house, with some of the walls removed and shelves put in. And books. And china and silver in display cases over there. And exotic lamps. And very fine paintings for sale and very old magazines that are not. All of this inside the shell of a house sitting beside other houses on a street that is not a commercial street. And so I naturally wonder if I am in the right place. For the right reasons. Do you have children, Miss Meyer?"

"What do you want?"

"I'm part of a three-judge panel now, a sort of review board, examining old cases. Writing recommendations for the Judiciary Committee. Correcting a few old mistakes. I hope that doesn't shock you as profoundly as it shocks us. Three old fellows of the bar, occasionally stumbling over one of their own mistakes."

"What do you want?"

"The picture of course. That's the best I can do."

"The best that you can do?"

"Yes. We all agreed. It was a mistake. Far outside the sentencing guidelines, even ten or twelve years ago. The newspapers loved it of course. There were clippings. But poetic justice isn't justice, and it was in fact a mistake. That's the reason I've come myself. To tell you that your sentence, the terms of your probation, have been reviewed and set aside. Officially." He took a long envelope from the inner pocket of his coat and passed it to me.

For a long time I said nothing. Did not open the envelope or even touch it where it lay.

I looked at it and wondered what he expected me to do.

Weird Tales, October 1933, Volume 22, Number 4. $625. Cover illustration by Margaret Brundage. Lead story "The Vampire Master" by Hugh Davidson, a novel, part one of four. Overall VG to Fine condition. Cover background lime green to forest green to dark green, mottled (in orig. illus.) but no fading. No splits or tears. All pages intact. No flaking or chipping. No tape. No marks. Purchased at auction.

This is the famous "bat girl" cover by Brundage.

I keep it in the cabinet beside the display case because it is so rare.

She is dressed in black and wearing a mask that covers the upper half of her face. Some collectors have suggested that it is a Halloween mask because the cover was published in October, but I believe it is more than a mask. It is a crown or a helmet, fitting over the skull like a second skin and spreading itself at the top into the image of a bat, its outstretched wings suggesting a hovering menace like the hooded cobra of a pharaoh's crown. And the subtle decadence of the dress she wears, high collared and tight around the throat, shining like black satin and straining against her breasts, is as detailed as decadence could be in 1933. Sometimes the collectors come into my shop and ask for the one with the girl in the leather dress or the hooded halter, you know, the one with the arms like this.

And that is what they want, the arms in a most peculiar pose. Raised, elbows high, with forearms angled down, almost into an inverted V, so that the backs of her hands lightly touch her face. Which suggests, somehow, a world of sensuous flesh. They see it too in her mouth, the lips parted and curved like an unbent bow, innocent of any smile. And the eyes, of course, as black and vacant as the abyss. Has she been caught, we want to know, in a moment of drunken lassitude; or could we see, somewhere off the sheet, that she has been pinned like an exotic moth against the green velvet, dying by degrees, like one of Scott Fitzgerald's tubercular wives.

They all know that any cover by Margaret Brundage is valuable. The sylph-like girls on every one of them are uncomfortably real and fragile, giving the impression of having been drawn from living models. Indeed, it's surprising that she became the most collected artist of the pulp era given the fantastic excesses of her competitors. Her own covers have little depth or background, and her lines, having been first set down in pastels, did not translate well to print, especially considering the primitive technology of the time. In style they resemble the drawings found in fashion magazines. Often there would be only a single detail separating Brundage's world from that of *Harper's Bazaar*—a ballerina dancing with a severed skull, a harem girl with a whip. From 1929 until 1938 she was the only female artist in the world producing art for the pulp market, and yet during those years she had a virtual monopoly on the covers for *Weird Tales*. Today they are called fetish covers and are collected by people who have never read the stories of Lovecraft or Howard, Clark Ashton Smith or Seabury Quinn. They are now what they were then, splashes of color in monochromatic lives, frail treasures in red and green, and black and gold, and yellow and blue.

In the future. We will go looking for the rocket cars in red and green, skimming from dome to dome. Which one is our city? That is what we will want to know. And our elevator to Mars? Where are the autopilots and happy passengers? And where have we berthed the space yachts with their light sails billowing like *Cutty Sark* and their teenagers racing around the sun? The gyrocopter in the garage and the robot dog at night? Where did they go? We have been promised for decades our floating house with foam furniture and never-aging skin, or at least a cream to set the wrinkles right. Picnics on some Sea of Tranquility with our rocket engineer and our android child, plucking meteors like peaches. Reminiscing of Earth our home. They seem to have all gone missing. Every storied issue of "Life in the Year 2000" has been confiscated, lost, compacted with the trash of the last millennium. And we're on our own.

That's why I have my shop. I lay the covers out like this because they send the only signal that I know. I try to show them with "The Black God's Kiss" that she'd willingly embrace, set her mouth to cold obsidian and insinuate her hips beneath the folds of his darkened robe. But no. It's a still life after all. His eyes are hooded hawks, and in his squatting pose the graceless hands grasp only at his graceless feet. It's a statue and not a god. While her insistent curvature shouts, "Look at me, the pretty one. Look at me. Perfectly preserved. In glass."

In other words, I give them the perfect truth, that nothing ever happens on our covers. The sword is raised but forever stayed. Beauty really rendered into art within some frozen vat. Because the story is ever undercover, and in between the words of brittle pages. We do not thumb them, I have found, when we know they will flutter to the floor.

So I wait for some pioneer to break the mold, some intergalactic ranger perhaps, who will slip between dimensions and find my little shop. Sometimes they do, making furtive visits before their energy abates, lingering like a man looking for the lost jewels of . . . some childish, imaginary place. And maybe once a year the boldest one will ask, "Are you the one? Who collected all of these? Because the sign outside . . ."

"Doesn't list my name," I will say.

And then he will fumble, adding, "Oh yeah. What I mean is, someone gave me your card. And I was wondering . . ."

Or perhaps he will explore. Buy a few titles from the mundane shelves, the ones that keep me in bread and milk, making himself familiar with the territory, before drifting into the happy aisles. Twisting his wedding band the way they do, looking up and down to make sure we are alone before suggesting, "Are you the one? Who collected all of these? Because the sign outside . . ."

"Doesn't list my name."

"Doesn't list your name," this special one will say. But I can sense the need behind his wooden words. It's maybe once a year, or maybe once in every two, when one of them will take the extra step. "Though it's just . . . such a great name for a bookstore. Why, when I was a kid, I could spend days in a place like this."

And "Pulp Life?" I will say. "You like my name? Well, thank you. You're very kind to notice."

"Yeah. Someone gave me your card, you know, told me about this place. And I was wondering. Do you have some more? Some items, I mean, that you might not have out here. To build a collection around."

It's the moment that I encourage him, step close enough to study the brown hair flecked with gray and brown eyes set beneath a wide, intelligent brow, like one of those descriptions in Edgar Allan Poe. And even if it's summer, he will wear his tie, carry his sports coat over the sleeve of his blue-checked shirt. And probably I will think he is English because his diction will be so precise and because he's one of the gentle ones determined not to show his wounds. With an aura of expensive aftershave. A slight fraying at the cuffs. "What do you have in mind?"

And he will say, "I'm not sure, in fact. I thought I just might look. If you had some more like these. It seems like I'm recapturing part of my sordid past." And he will laugh an awkward laugh.

"Yes. A few. Back here," and I will laugh as well, touching his arm like this to show a slight embarrassment, "in the back bedroom." But of course there will be tables and shelves as well as lamps and chairs. All completely safe. And if, at the end of the afternoon, we have found what we both will need, then we sit in silent union for maybe an hour more. Turning pages that crumble as we read. Mouthing words that keep us home to stay.

ONE WHO GOT AWAY

Escape

1

It's so steep at the crest that Rifken can simply lean forward, and the snow holds, as pliable and comforting as a blanket. He works a hollow among the boulders and waits, drinking in the thin air. There are no tree limbs between him and the white moon. And there is no more to the mountain, no higher ridge to supply perspective. There is just the momentary illusion that he is back at his grandfather's farm, looking down upon a floating disk at the bottom of a stone well. The only movement comes from Hargadon, the younger deputy, thirty yards below in the frozen present and still climbing with undiminished energy. It takes the kid several minutes to scramble past and then edge up to the ridge itself, where he takes out binoculars and tries to read their future.

"If you're going to do that," murmurs Rifken, "may as well stand up and wave a flag."

Wind rakes powder from their ledge and scatters it over the valley. Hargadon hunches lower, crabbing backward onto a shallow shelf made by his feet. "It's still dark," he says. "He couldn't have seen me."

"There's a moon. And there's snow."

"Hell, I don't know. I don't even know what day it is anymore. It's so damn cold I can't feel a thing. I can't even think." Hargadon slips off a mitten to cup his bare hand over nose and mouth, puffing four, five breaths while the vapor rises between his fingers.

"He's down there, isn't he?" Rifken tries to see in his mind what's on the other side of the ridge.

"This can't be real, man. They quit making this kinda movie a long, long time ago. Your people just not get the message or something?"

"We got the message. Is he down there or not?"

"You're a throwback, Rifken, you know that? You're in the wrong century. You and him both. You're driving us all nuts. Two hundred state troopers, seventy-five local cops, twenty of us from Windfield. And two crazy Indians. You and him. Do you hate us that much, Rifken? Is this part of some master plan?"

"Tell me. What did you see?"

For a long time Hargadon says nothing. Finally maneuvers the rifle sheath around to his front and lies back in the snow, gazing at distant stars. Then, without looking down, he draws a cartridge clip from inside his parka, testing the spring with one finger. Then he slips his rifle from its sheath, rolls onto his side and inserts the clip, sliding the bolt back and forth to chamber a round. And raises both lens covers from the telescopic sight. Then answers, "I saw the son of a bitch. Standing in the middle of a lake."

Rifken waits, settling the image in his mind, trying to believe.

"I swear to God I could go to sleep right here. I could die happy this minute. Except, you know what?" Hargadon unhooks the binoculars and passes them to the older deputy. "Except then, Rifken, I'd never know what you crazy bastards did next."

Rifken props the binoculars on a crust of snow and studies the circular scene below him on the dark side of the ridge. After an age he says, "Let's go."

Finally.

They begin their delicate dance, separating on the downslope, picking their way among dead trees and ragged stumps that look like tombstones. Rifken wonders what kind of magic could kill an entire forest, leave it looking like the crumbling pillars of a lost civilization. And he worries about creaking snow and skeletal branches under the white powder, any silly sound that could crack the surface of things and set Robert James Henley to flight again. And instead of the brittle wind, he feels the cold emptiness inside of himself that, years ago, replaced the medicine pouch given to him by his grandfather. He makes a slow descent like a hunter, eyes intently upon a man who, just as the kid said, is standing in the middle of a shallow lake.

A man neither fishing nor swimming, but simply exhaling great triangular clouds of fear like a horse standing and stamping as wolves gather. Around a glistening secret lake so sharply cold and dense that the man seems to have been cut at the knees. Wisps of steam drifting above the snowmelt. So that when the figure finally begins to wade, it leaves a shimmering trail of silver like a ghost.

Forty yards upslope, among white riblike branches, Hargadon waits for something to happen, squinting through the telescopic sight of his match rifle, trying to hold steady in the cold, and wondering what is taking his partner so long. Thinking, man, this is crazy. This doesn't make a lick of sense.

While Rifken watches, working through the legends, trying to remember the old stories, his lips even forming some of the words or maybe a prayer, answered only by snowflakes drifting down through the darkness, that touch the hard reflective water, darken, and disappear.

Then the wading man reaches shore, his coppery hand giving no ripple as it cups the water, and only the faintest lip-lip as he raises it dripping and draws three fingers across his cheek. And then nothing. The end of the spell perhaps, with Rifken rising out of his squat and taking a step forward, further scattering the moment with his flat Appalachian accent. "Robert-James, is that you?"

The man doesn't even turn. "*Ataghi.*"

"It's me and Hargadon."

"Ah. I figured it might be."

"You about ready now? It's plumb cold, and we got a ways to walk."

Now Hargadon comes carelessly down through cracked limbs and snowdrifts, cradling the rifle, fitting fingers back into his thick ski mittens. "You got that right." Then to the prisoner, "Jeezus Christ, Henley, what were you doing in the middle of a lake? It's a helluva night for froggin', ain't it?"

Rifken gives him a distant look, nods toward the east where the slope is gentle. They work their way back to the trail in zigzags, skirting the ravines and thickets, following the last of the animal tracks where they can. Within minutes Henley's jeans have stiffened and turned gray-white below the thighs.

"He's gonna be frostbit 'fore we get back to the truck, and I ain't carrying his ass down no mountain—you might wanna think about that, Chief. We not gonna cuff him or anything?"

Rifken takes off his gloves, thrusts them at Henley. To Hargadon he says, "Son—it's cold. It's night. And we got a ways to go. Why don't you just drop back a few steps and keep your finger on the trigger if that'd make it more official in your mind."

"I might just do that. How about you, Henley? You mind if I keep the crosshairs on you for a while?"

"I don't much care."

"Well, what about your buddy Willie T? Way I figure it, today or tomorrow's gotta be the day. Your very large neighbor on D Block might be nice and toasty warm about now. Does that have any appeal to you, Henley? It does to me."

"Why are you talking like this?" says Rifken. "What's wrong with you?"

"Jeezus, Rifken! You're making me nervous. Kind of glad I'm the one with the gun." The two Indians stop and together stare at Hargadon, who takes a step back. "I don't like weirdness, man. And that's what we got here. I mean, help me out, Henley, you do know that you're an escaped murderer, don't you? I'm not going to wake up in a few minutes with the big headache and blankets on the floor, am I?"

Henley stares. Rifken turns and continues down the ridge, breaking trail.

"Okay then. But just tell me one thing, I mean if it don't trouble you too much. What the hell you doing in the middle of a pond a freezing water?"

"I don't remember," says Henley.

2

They are four hours from the truck when it begins to sleet.

At first Hargadon thinks it might be a warm rain drifting up from the Gulf since he feels the familiar tapping on his shoulder and hears the patter. But there are no pocks in the snow, and the air has begun to hiss like dry aspen. Soon enough he notices tiny ice particles bouncing off the scope of his rifle and, after a time, more particles clinging to the smooth blue barrel. It takes another indefinite distance along a narrow ledge for the stomach-fear to hit him and for him to realize that he has heard this sound before — in the warm, safe summer — when you kick over a rock and discover a nest of rattlers. It's a picture so vivid and a feeling so strong that for a moment Hargadon stares absurdly at the rocky outcroppings all around him, unmoving until a fresh gust reminds him that the only rattlers are safe below ground. He shakes the idea out of his mind, resheaths the rifle, and closes the gap between himself and Henley, looking back only once and noticing how the sleet gradually obscures the trail behind him. Then goes hurrying after the two silent figures ahead of him as they traverse a saddleback and cross two low ridges before heading back up toward gathering clouds.

"Hey, Rifken, you know what? There might be a bounty on this guy. I mean, I know we don't get a real bounty but maybe a little recognition, you know, like some time off or something. A little palm trees and sand, that's what I'm thinking about. Some place warm. Hell, I'd settle for a cup of hot coffee right this minute, you know what I mean? You got any hot coffee up there? Hey! I'm talking to you."

Rifken finds a gray-white boulder with enough of an overhang for the three of them, then waits for the two younger men to catch up. "I got part of a sandwich," he says, "and a little sip of water," ignoring whatever it is that Hargadon is saying as he slides against the lichen-crusted rock and settles into a tight tuck next to Henley. Instead, Rifken takes a long-barreled flashlight from his pack and studies the prisoner's face. Touches the ears and cheek with his bare hand. "Give him your scarf," he says to Hargadon.

"What?"

"Give him your scarf. And anything else you can spare."

Hargadon unwinds the scarf and helps to wrap Henley's ears and face. "Man, what the hell did any of us do to deserve this?"

"I'm sorry," the prisoner says. "I didn't expect to get this far."

"Yeah? Well, have a drink of water—or have you already had enough of that for one night?"

"I'm fine. I'm not even cold."

"We need to keep moving," says Rifken.

"What we need is a damn fire, or a radio that works."

"If we drop down into those trees, we won't find any dry wood, and we'll be lost in an hour. Best to stick to the high route." He plays the flashlight out over the void and watches the light scatter among sparkling droplets of ice. "And even if your radio did work . . . , who do you think's going to helicopter you out of here tonight?"

"Yeah, well, this ain't the way we came in."

"I know."

"You *are* Cherokee, right?"

"Enough."

"What I mean is, you know where we are. Right?"

"There." Rifken nods toward a ragged silhouette that looks like the edge of the earth. "That's where we're headed."

"Jesus Christ. This is crazy. The hunting part is over, man. We got him. Or haven't you figured that out yet?"

"Look, you've done all right so far. You got nothing to be ashamed of."

"But what?"

"But we've got a rough spell ahead. And a few hours yet before dawn."

Hargadon is surprised at how difficult it is to stand. He has to leverage himself to his feet and pull upright using handholds in the rock. As he rubs circulation back into legs, he notices that Henley has not moved, that he is still propped against a pillowlike stone with his feet already covered by a filmy blanket of sleet and snow. The white scarf has come loose from his head and fallen about his neck so that it looks casual, like a proper scarf, with one end draped over his shoulder and the other hanging down like a tie. His breathing is low and regular, like a man about to fall asleep, and his arms lie limp, not clenched against the cold. From the thigh down, his jeans are black ice.

Rifken kneels and begins to massage him awake. "Help me get him up."

"What's wrong?"

They rewrap the scarf and get Henley moving toward the black rocks ahead. Then, after they have climbed another hundred feet, Rifken answers. "I think he's dying."

And gradually, like the cold night itself that seems to be working its way through the layers and folds of his clothing, a realization reaches Hargadon. That they are not headed back toward the truck. That the two hundred state troopers and seventy-five local police and eighteen deputized guards from Windfield are somewhere safe and warm in a world far below. And that what Rifken really means is that all three of them are dying. Like it was part of a plan.

In his mind Hargadon drifts away from the trail trying to make sense of what is happening. It's hard work. The thinking is as slow as walking. But finally it comes to him. He closes his eyes and backtracks over the past several hours, reading the signs and at last making his way to a half-formed idea. That Rifken is doing this on purpose. That he's going to let them die, the three of them, rather than take Henley back. Like it was some kind of Indian thing. It's an idea that grows more obvious and definite the closer he gets to it. Until finally Hargadon can open his eyes and look down at his own legs, coated with a powdery snow like pollen on a bee, and realize that he's following two dead men into oblivion. It's hard to think otherwise. The cold is like a weight pulling him down. He tries to blink his way back to consciousness, but the eyelids creak up and down without revealing any fork in the trail. Thinking Rifken will kill us if I don't do something. It's such an elegant answer to the riddling night that Hargadon can almost admire the way Rifken glides through the snow without lifting his feet. Or leaving tracks. As if he's skiing an inch or two below the surface. So that there is only a ruffled wake where he has gone and, after a few minutes, hardly a hint that he has passed this way at all.

3

It's still dark when they stop to rest again, this time beside the bank of a frozen stream where the water has been caught spurting from the mountain. The layers of ice look like a stepwork of nickels and quarters, but there is also a dry horseshoe of rock where Hargadon scrapes together some leaves and works to light a fire. With his last match he produces a minute's worth of smoke and despair. And then silence—a black and bottomless crevasse from which he contemplates Rifken who, suddenly and inexplicably, has turned talkative.

"Pure mountain honey," he says. "You can't go a hundred yards along any of those roads down there without seeing a sign that says pure mountain honey. That's what I'd give a million dollars for right now."

They are closer to the treeline now, the soggy pine needles and all the useless lumber of a national forest. From where they sit the trees swell up like an angry ocean, and Hargadon looks upon the sloping branches like a man who has been given his choice of ways to die, withdrawing deeper and deeper into his own thoughts. Verifying that everything Rifken has done for the past hour has been insane—massaging Henley like a fallen horse, stuffing frozen moss into the man's shirt, babbling about pure mountain honey. It's enough to make Hargadon shift his weight and work the rifle around to his side, casually, without seeming to think about the still-chambered round. Or the possibility of getting off two shots rather than just one.

"We need fuel more than we need fire, kid. How do you think the Eskimos do it? How do you think the ancestors did it? Here, help me get his boots off."

Hargadon narrows his eyes and retreats further into the abyss, until soon Rifken is only a speck and Henley has become one of the ageless boulders lying scattered on the side of the mountain. And there is a certain peace, though from very far away he can still hear Rifken's patter, a low, dangerous chant that tempts him back out into the frozen night, away from the warm place he has found, where he can listen without moving.

". . . grew up with my grandfather, who lived in a slab cabin just outside the reservation. Had an open well down the hill a ways where you could draw water from one of the underground streams that popped out of the mountain farther down, like this one here. Cold and clean all year round. You could lean over and see your own reflection, or the moon sometimes, as long as you didn't lean too far. Anyhow, he never set foot on government land—that's what he called the reservation—and he always made the people come to him when they needed something. You know, the healing. Are you hearing me, Hargadon? I'm trying to tell you something. I'm trying to tell you where we are."

The stars have reappeared, faint pinpricks of light that glow in the shifting haze. The sleeting has stopped or perhaps drifted down the mountain to glaze the world below. But neither Henley nor Hargadon has moved, and Rifken is making frantic motions over the bare legs and feet of the one while glancing from time to time at the other.

"Anyway, this part I'm telling you now . . . , it's like a myth. Which the people don't tell too often because they are practically all Baptists and such, going to church just like the white folks, except for my grandfather, who was a holy man. And really believed. So you can guess what it was like growing up in a cabin, no other man around, and my mama so grateful when the preacher from the reservation brought us a kerosene heater and a Christmas ham, and my grandfather telling me on the same day that the name of the place was *Ataghi*. And that it was sacred. Way far west, as far as you can go and still be in the mountains. Toward the red sun—that's the way he said it—so far into the mountains that only the animals knew the path. And that no hunter had ever seen it because of the magic. Like he wanted me to believe too. Telling me that even though there are lots of trails along the headwaters of the Oconaluftee—ones that go higher and higher into wild places—they get all tangled so that not even a little girl could crawl on her hands and knees. Only the animals know the way. Because it's a lake of magic water where no hunter ever walked the shore or drank from the streams that feed it. But sometimes, if a lost hunter would come near, there might be a big fluttering sound of wings and clouds of ducks and geese and doves and pigeons. Though if he ever reached the spot, there would be nothing, only a flat bed of earth and stone. Which is where we are now. Hargadon? We don't have that much farther to go. Just an hour. We can make it, all three of us."

Rifken has taken off his coat and wrapped Henley's legs as he continues to rub. When he finally looks up, he sees that Hargadon is still capable of moving and that—although he is still seated, still outwardly motionless—somehow the rifle has been unsheathed, and the mittens have been removed, and the dead eyes have reawakened with one final spark.

"Unless," says Rifken, "it was a spirit warrior who had first cleared his vision with a night of prayer and fasting. And even then he might see only faint tracks and a few feathers caught in the brambles. Maybe not even a blade of grass. So that most of the human beings in every age think that the lake dried up long ago, but that is not true either. It can appear, *Ataghi*, just at daybreak, to someone who has fasted all night and kept watch, Hargadon. Like a mirror of pure water. Shallow on the land but full of fish and reptiles, covered with water birds, while on the shore will be every kind of forest animal. Because it is the medicine lake of the beasts. And whenever the deer or the bear is wounded by a hunter, he makes his way along these trails, right here, up the headwaters to the secret place and wades into the pure water, swimming to the other side. And when he comes out, his wounds are healed. That's why the animals keep it hidden, this lake. Invisible. And that's the way it was told to me. When I was too young to know."

"Too young to know what?"

"Hargadon, listen to me. If you use that rifle, you'll never get out of here alive. I know where we are. I know how to get us out."

"I think you're looking for the same thing he was looking for."

"Maybe I am. But let me tell you something. Let me tell you why he's here."

"Him? He killed somebody."

"He killed his wife and the man she was with. That's true. That's absolutely true. He went home one night, to the trailer where he lived, and took out a pistol, and fired nine times in the bedroom where he found them. That's the God's honest truth. But that's not why he's here. He's here because two of those shots went through a very flimsy wall in that trailer, Hargadon. A paper-thin wall. And on the other side of that wall was a little girl. That's why he's here. Because of something he didn't intend. That's what I want you to think about, firing a shot you don't intend."

"You don't have any idea where we are. You're just walking, hoping for a miracle."

"On the other side of that ridge is what you want. I swear. Just give us one more hour, and I'll have you where you need to be."

Hargadon raises the barrel slightly and clicks off the safety. Then raises it higher until the front sight is aimed at the moon and fires a shot into the air. Works the bolt without looking and fires another. And then a third. "There might be somebody out looking for us," he says. "You can never tell."

Snow falls from the limb of a spruce some thirty yards below them and sets off a cascade that clears the powder from one side of the tree. Then the uppermost branch bends again and launches a white owl that takes flight like a diver springing into the air, fluttering as it gathers the night beneath its wings and then settling into the slow rhythm of flight as it descends into the valley.

"Come on," says Rifken. "We're going to have to carry him now."

4

Henley stops breathing on the upslope and then, somewhere between the ravine and the second spur, dies without a sound. Hargadon can guess what has happened when the weight becomes easier to bear, more like a load of wood than a sack of meal. Still he keeps going because he knows what the news will do to Rifken. They go until a patch of loose gravel stops them. It's where Hargadon slips, loses his hold on Henley's arm, and the body planks into the snow. Rifken doesn't even look. He can do no more than bend at the waist and gasp, blowing out clouds of foggy breath like a spent runner. Finally he looks around to get his bearings before kneeling to feel for a pulse, as if it were all a foregone conclusion. After holding his fingers against Henley's throat for a moment, he says to no one in particular, "I can't hardly breathe anymore," then begins to pull off the gloves he gave Henley back at the lake.

The younger man watches Rifken work the gloves back onto his own gray hands as if they are magic. Then, when Rifken shivers and buries his hands beneath his arms, Hargadon is sure he has seen a sign. He tries to unfreeze his mind. "What now?" he says.

"I'll be honest with you. We ought to be able to see the town from here, the lights and all. Maybe the storm knocked out their power."

"That's not what I mean. What are we going to do about him?"

Rifken sits back on his haunches and rests his wrists on his knees. "I can't hardly breathe. Or think. You might be getting your wish after all—to walk out of here alone."

"Just rest a few minutes."

"Why do you all of a sudden care about him? I thought you wanted off this mountain as fast as you could get off."

"I don't know."

"Maybe you see yourself." The older man nods toward the body.

"No. He did wrong. But tried to get to the right place. You got to respect that, and maybe I wouldn't mind being back up here again myself when spring comes."

"Now who's crazy?"

"I'm just thinking out loud, that's all. Like we did what we had to do. And so did he."

"It wasn't real, kid. It was just a lake."

"Yeah. I know. But if this body was to slip into a ravine or something, it probably wouldn't be found. Maybe ever. And then he might get whatever it is he was looking for. I'm just wondering is all. Wondering if there's something we owe, me and you. Like a debt that needs repaying. Anyway—I'll tell you one thing for sure. I don't have it in me to carry him over that ridge. And neither do you."

Rifken rubs his face and sinks lower into himself, remembering how grateful his mother had been for heat and food. How that preacher, a Cherokee man himself, had treated them with respect, talking low and humble, without any hurry in the world until the day he said, "Miz Rifken, you ever thought about being saved?"

Hargadon unzips the parka and drapes it over the seated figure, stamping his boots clean before climbing a few steps higher to where a massive rockface meets the narrow trail. "All I know is you're the one who seems to have a problem with this, not me." He finds a wide foothold and works his way up to a vertical split.

"What the hell are you doing?" Rifken stands, letting the second parka fall at his feet.

"I just thought that if one of us could make it up to that table rock, he could probably see if the road was down there. And that the other one could stay here . . . do what needed doing . . . and then take the trail around and down." He inserts one foot into the slit and pulls with both hands until his knee finds a six-inch ledge. Then the fingers read the rock above his head and discover another handhold. He moves like a mechanical spider, slowly, feeling his way with all four limbs and keeping his body flat against the wrinkled surface. When he slips, he does not gasp or flail but simply pulls himself along as if climbing and falling were inseparable halves of the same thing. At the top Hargadon is no more than thirty feet from where he has started, but he falls forward and promises himself sleep, enough sleep for a lifetime, if he can just be allowed to see beneath the first painful sliver of light breaking beyond the next range. He takes one last breath, then stands on the tabletop and shades his eyes.

While from below an old man's voice drifts up to him. "What do you see? Is there a cut bank and a stand of hemlock?"

"Yeah," says Hargadon. "Yeah, there is. And I can see the road too."

5

The truck is nearly covered under a mound of snow, but it starts as soon as Hargadon turns the key. For a few minutes he sits with his head bowed and his arms draped over the steering wheel, unmoving even though the first cold air from the heater stings his hands. Ice crystals in his three-day stubble begin to melt and trickle to the point of his chin. Still he doesn't move, drinking in the growing warmth like a greenhouse orchid and gradually opening to the possibilities of the new day. The seat cover, after two days in the storm, creaks every time he breathes; but the engine revs, and the radio works. So Hargadon stretches one or two muscles at a time and listens to the reports coming in from the first patrols headed back up into the mountains. Then he switches to a country music station and waits.

Looking out the passenger window he can see Windfield itself, gray as a castle and crowning the crest of the next range. It does not look like a prison. It is something more human, a cathedral perhaps, or a Tibetan lamasery, or refuge for the penitent, just above the level of clouds. There are no fences or guard towers. No rats or damp, dripping pipes in Windfield. It is clean and warm. He knows because, on most days, he works there with his friend Rifken and the others. Where the greenery, just outside the walls, is so thick and tangled you cannot run in a straight line, could not fall or fly or even skitter like loose stone down to the towns below.

Hargadon turns the defroster on high and steps out of the truck to begin brushing the snow away from the windshield with his arm. He hears a hissing sound behind him and turns to see a car from the state patrol. It rolls to a stop, idling with a low growl as the driver makes a quick radio call. Then steps out on the far side. He is a tall black man with close-cropped hair and a starched gray uniform. Campaign hat and polished boots. Jacket open and clear of his holster. "You doing all right?" he asks.

Hargadon sees him eyeing the Department of Corrections decal on the side of the truck. "Doing okay now. Had a hard night of it though."

"You wouldn't be one of those missing guards, would you? From Windfield?"

"Yeah. I'm Hargadon."

"You look like you been through it."

"Yeah, well . . . it got a little tricky."

"They're looking for you about as hard as they're looking for Henley." The trooper turns and regards the ragged furrow in the snow leading back up the side of the mountain. "You find anything?"

"Yeah. Rocks and snow."

"What about the other one?"

"Rifken? We split up about an hour ago. I came over the top; he's working his way around the ridge."

"I'd call in if I was you. Anyhow, I'm headed up to the roadblock on 321. You need anything?"

"No," says Hargadon. "We're headed in."

The trooper steps through the just-softening snow to his car and guns the engine before driving away. Hargadon follows with his eyes, noticing how the slush holds the impression of the tires and how the sun has found one or two patches of asphalt. The windows of the patrol car glisten as it recedes, and the engine fades to a soft purr, and then to nothing. There is only a clean, cold rush from the valley. As the car disappears around the last curve, Hargadon takes a long draft of pure mountain air and lets his eyes wander from the road. Up to the stand of hemlocks where he sees white movement, a bent branch, and a cascade of snow. Like a great white owl taking flight.

The Flannery O'Connor Award for Short Fiction